Evelyn Raymond

The Little Lady of the Horse

Evelyn Raymond

The Little Lady of the Horse

ISBN/EAN: 9783337118839

Printed in Europe, USA, Canada, Australia, Japan

Cover: Foto ©Andreas Hilbeck / pixelio.de

More available books at **www.hansebooks.com**

THE

LITTLE LADY OF THE HORSE

BY

EVELYN RAYMOND

BOSTON
ROBERTS BROTHERS
1894

THE

LITTLE LADY OF THE HORSE.

CHAPTER I.

SUTRO AND STEENIE.

SUTRO and young Steenie were where they might have been found on almost every day at the same hour, — down on the beach, where the great cañon cut through the *mesa* to the sea.

A group of rocks, roughly piled, and a few evergreen shrubs clustering about them, made a pleasant break in a long, monotonous stretch of coast, and the coolness of the spot was always refreshing after their canter in the sunshine. Their horses had been unsaddled

1

and set free to browse upon the herbage up the cañon; and these moved here and there, lazily, as if — like the old *caballero* himself — they felt the languor of that midday hour.

"Sutro, what makes the water so bluey-green?" asked the little girl, who had been sitting silent for full one minute and gazing dreamily at the shining waves.

"*Caramba!*   How can I tell?"

"But you should know, should n't you? Does n't everybody keep learning things all the time? If I were a'most a hundred, like you, I should know everything, I think. In verity, I should be able to answer a simple question such as that. And so I tell you."

"*Si?*   Thou wouldst find thou knew nothing at all, maybe; and thou wouldst not trouble if it were so. Because, if the good *Dios* wished to make us wise He would put wisdom into our heads without labor to us, would n't he? Why not?"

"Fie, my Sutro! Do I learn reading that way? But no. I should wait a long time first, my father says. Well, then, if you do not know what makes the water green, I s'pose, at least, you can tell what lies beyond the water?"

"Ah, that I can! Beyond the water lies tł sky. Thou canst see that for thyself," answere the old man, with a chuckle of delight, and pointing to the horizon, where, in truth, the sky and ocean seemed to blend.

"No, that is a mistake, begging your pardon, dear Sutro, though it looks so. For my father says that it is only seeming; and that if I were to sail 'way, 'way over ever so far, it would be just as it is here, — the water so low down and the sky so high up above my reach. But, dearie me, I s'pose you will never tell me anything, Sutro! I must find out all things for myself. I wish my father was n't so busy. I wish my mother had n't died when I was a baby. I wish I knew what makes the road-runners such silly birds. Why should they keep always in front of one in a chase after them? Why don't they fly up out of the way? But, of course, you can't tell. And I wish — I wish — What makes people grow wrinkley when they get old? You can't help being wrinkley, I know that, dear Sutro, but what makes it?"

"*En verdad!* It may be answering thy idle questions, Little Un; yet there is one thing I would have thee know, and remember it. My soul! if thou dost not, I will be — "

"Not angry, please, Sutro!" cried Steenie, in sudden alarm.

"Maybe no. Not angry, truly. But wilt thou remember? I cannot be a hundred till the *Natividad* (Christmas) comes round five-and-ten times more. When I am a hundred years, thou wilt be a woman. This I know, because I asked Father Antonio when I was last at his house. My father was a hundred and ten when he died; and his father even more than that. The Vives' family lives long in this world, and — *Guay!* wouldst thou lie down without thy blanket?"

For Steenie had thrown herself full length on the mass of sea-pink vines, and would have been asleep in another moment; but kind old Sutro spread his gay Navajo blanket further up, under the shelter of the rocks, and, after the child had curled herself upon it, arranged with utmost care the branches of the chaparral till she was wholly screened from sunlight. Next, he whistled for the horses, who came obediently back to the mouth of the cañon; and then he went speedily to sleep, as Steenie had done. But for himself he made no screen, save his arm across his eyes, nor any bed softer than the warm sand.

During the next half hour these two odd comrades slumbered so peacefully that the teal in the pool beyond the rocks, and the sand-pipers in the rushes, went on about their business as fear-

lessly as if no human intruders were near; but
when the half-hour was up, the girl awoke as
suddenly as she had slept. Sitting on her blanket, she pushed her brown curls from her blue
eyes, and looked mischievously around at old
Sutro, whom she began to pelt with the crimson-
rayed pinks, aiming so deftly that one gold-
hearted blossom landed plump in the open mouth
of the sleeper. "*Hola! hola!* that was well
sent!" shouted she.

Sputtering the flower from his lips, the Spaniard retorted, "In verity, I — "

But if he meant to scold his darling he was
not allowed; for she leaned over him, patted his
brown cheeks, and kissed him squarely on the
forehead, in the very thickest tangle of the wrin-
kles she so disliked. "There, there, that will
do, Señor Sutro Vives! If I was rude, you
will forgive me; and if I hurt you, the wound
will heal."

"Thou hast healed it already, Little Un, and
hast gladdened the heart of thy slave!" answered
the other, with the extravagance of expression to
which his tongue was prone.

"Pooh, my Sutro, you my slave, — the proud-
est of proud on all Santa Felisa ranch! My
father says that the blood of three races runs

in your veins, and that you have kept the best part of each. What does he mean by that? I heard him talking thus, once, with some strangers, who came to see the place. It was when you rode away on Mazan', there; and one of the gentlemen said you were a very picture-y, or something, kind of a man, and — "

"Ten thousand pardons, Little Un, but it is false!"

"Why, Sutro, what do you mean? Is n't it fine to be picture-y? I 'm sure the stranger thought so, for he noticed everything about you, — your buckskin leggings, your sombrero, your big saddle, your lariat, and all. He said you were a most int'resting kind of a 'type,' and an 'old Californian,' and so on. I did n't like the 'old' part of the talk, though, 'cause if you have to be called old, I 'd rather do it myself, would n't I?"

Sutro vouchsafed no reply. His brow had grown moody, and his movements betokened anger; for he picked up the blanket, and folded it with unusual precision, and, if it were possible, threw his shoulders back more squarely than ever. At that moment, from the snap of his black eyes and the rigidity of his upright figure, he might have been eighteen instead of eighty-five, which was the number of years Father Antonio's reckoning accorded him.

Steenie became silent, for the one thing she feared was anger; but when the *caballero* whistled for Mazan', she puckered her own red lips into a summons for Tito, who answered by a loving neigh and an immediate approach.

Not so the brown mare, Mazan', to whose sensitive ears Sutro's whistle had conveyed the information that her master was cross; and when that was the case, it were well that all tender-hearted creatures kept out of his way. So, instead of trotting forward to be mounted, pretty Mazan' trotted off up the beach, and at a distance of a few rods broke into a wild gallop toward home.

Then Steenie laughed; she couldn't help it, though she trembled instantly, fearing she had made matters worse.

But no. There was something so merry and infectious about that laugh that doting old Sutro was not the one to withstand its influence; his frown relaxed to a smile. "Well, well, *En verdad!* Mazan knows something after all! For she would be a foolish thing to come back for a beating she did not deserve, would she not, *mi nina* [my little one]?"

"So I should think, indeed! But what fun! You shall mount with me, and we will chase her. She'll not stop to think that Tito can run her two to one, will she?"

"No, no!" assented the *caballero*, vaulting up behind his young favorite, and making ready for use the lariat which had been wound around his waist while he rested; also, for once, accepting without challenge Steenie's declaration that Tito was the fleeter animal.

Such a race as that was! Save themselves and the fleeing mare, not a moving thing was in sight; for, leaving the *mesa* bluff and the cañon, they left also the teal and the sand-pipers and the few creeping creatures which lived in the chaparral. To the west glittered the rich-hued Pacific Ocean; before them and behind them lay miles and miles of yellow beach, while far eastward towered the mountains which formed the boundary of the great Santa Felisa rancho.

Lonely? Why, yes, it may have been; but so free, so roomy, and so sunny, that these two who darted athwart the picture never thought of loneliness. Besides, why should they? Santa Felisa was home to them; and during the few short years that Steenie Calthorp had lived she had viewed just such wide stretches of this lovely

world, and no other; for a city, or even town,
she had never seen.

As they rode they talked, — the girl asking
and her attendant parrying questions without
number, till he cried out, impatiently, "If thou
wilt chatter always, Little Un, how can Tito win
the race? Be quiet now, for just two minutes,
and my lady Mazan' shall feel the rope about her
throat, if Sutro's hand has not lost its cunning,
with all this tiresome talk of 'old,' 'old'!"

"*Ce, ce, ce!*" echoed Steenie, softly, in her
eagerness using the familiar Spanish injunction
to silence, and bending low to whisper a few
encouraging words in Tito's ear. Like an arrow
he shot forward, and in a brief space had gained
so close to Mazan' that Sutro made ready to
throw.

"Whiz-z! Swish!" The rope had cut the air
in shining circles above the runaway's straining
head, and descended with unerring exactness to
her steaming neck; who, at the first touch of the
cord, understood its meaning, and stood stock-
still, — a throbbing, beautiful, but wholly conquered thing.

"*Caramba!* Señ'rita Mazan'! Wouldst serve
thy master so? Take that —"

But the uplifted hand was stayed, as suddenly

as the mare's flight had been, by Steenie's clutch of Sutro's wrist, and her rebuke : "What! would you strike her, really, — Mazan', who never knew stroke or blow! Or has this been your habit, and I s'posing you so gentle! For shame to you, Sutro Vives! and shame ten thousand times! What is she but — "

"A vixen! so I tell thee, who must be broken of her evil tricks. *Caramba !* Thus I will have it. 'Women and mares and a spaniel dog — '"

".Sutro! Leave your dirty Spanish jabbering, and listen to me. If you strike her you shall not ride on the beach — for — one — whole — week! And ' so I tell thee ' ! I will take — let me see — maybe Nicoloso Barbazon, instead."

" *Si ?* but thou wilt not, Little Un! What does the stupid Nicoloso know of what a señorita's body-servant should be ? Answer me that. *Caramba !* "

" Ah, ha, my Sutro! Somebody is silly still; but it is n't Mazan', nor Tito, nor me! And you make me think you are not well : you are so very, very cross. Never mind, poor thing! Get upon your pretty beast, who stands so quiet now, and let us go on. I am as hungry as hungry; are n't you ? "

" But — Nicoloso ? "

" Pooh ! for Nicoloso ! He need n't come if you
are good, need he ? Sutro, what makes one so
uncomf'table to be hungry ? If it were n't for that
queerness inside of me I could stay out all day,
and maybe all night."

" Ten thousand pardons, Señ'rita, but thou
couldst not. What would thy father do if dinner
came but not his little daughter ? "

" Sure — what could he ? He could n't live
without me, could he ? And there's the house.
Another race, 'tween Tito and Mazan' this time,
not Tito catching her. To the house. I'll beat
you, my Sutro ! "

They struck into it briskly ; but, as they neared
the goal, both riders slackened pace at sight of a
strange carriage standing before the ranch-house
door, with several of the household servants
grouped excitedly about it.

" More strangers ! " cried Steenie, regretfully.
" It is nothing but comp'ny all the time, nowa-
days ; and I get no more nice times with papa,
because he must always attend to them. I wish
they would n't come ; don't you, Sutro ? "

But she received no answer ; for the old *caballero*
had muttered two words, " The master ! " then had
dashed around the building toward the kitchen court.

" The master ? Who can he be ? Is n't my

father the master? Except, of course, that great rich lord who owns Santa Felisa, and never comes near it at all, — not once in all my life, my father says; and I 'm sure I hope he has n't now, for I should be dreadfully afraid of a lord who wore a gold cor'net on his head, as Suzan' says 'every lord does who is any 'count at all.'"

But he had indeed come; and the little girl, who had trotted slowly up to the verandah, was lifted from her saddle, and duly presented by her father, the manager, to a stout, red-faced old gentleman as, "My Lord, my daughter."

"So? Hm-m. Let me see. Wife died. Only one? So, so. Nice child. Run along, Sissy. Hm-m. I'd like dinner now. Great country for appetite — California. Afterward, business."

Mr. Calthorp bowed gravely and respectfully; and, loosing Steenie's hand, bade her make herself ready for the table as soon as possible. She held up her face for a kiss, then sped away, thinking she had never seen her father look so serious, and wondering why. "Was he afraid of a lord, too? And was the cor'net under the man's hat?" ⸙

Customs were simple at Santa Felisa; for, till now, the household had been practically that of the manager alone, and, in default of an older person, Daniel Calthorp had liked to have his little

daughter preside at table. So it seemed strange
to none but Lord Plunkett himself when, a little
later than usual, she entered the dining-room and
took her usual place. Feeling she must honor
such a wonderful occasion, she had taken uncom-
mon pains with her toilet; and, fortunately, the
guest was too indifferent to such matters to be
shocked by the rather striking combination of a
red sash, a blue throat-knot against the white
frock, and a mass of reddish-brown curls bound
into a stiff little knot by a band of green velvet.

Sutro followed her. As the oldest resident of
the rancho, he felt that he fully understood the
requirements of the hour; and he had also hastily
arrayed himself in his gayest apparel, to take his
place solemnly behind his little " señorita's "
chair. There he stood, perfectly motionless, apparently not noticing anybody, — even Steenie
herself, — and reminding the amused Lord Plunkett of nothing in the world save one of the wooden
figures outside a tobacconist's shop.

A Chinese waiter, instructed and assisted by the
valet, Dorsey, served the unexpected guest, and
the housemaid attended to the others. But nobody ate very much except the stranger; for Mr.
Calthorp was too busy answering his lordship's
questions, and Steenie too curiously regarding his
lordship's appearance.

Suddenly that gentleman looked up. " Well, Sissy! What d' ye think? Seem to be staring sharp. Children read folks. Hope you 'll like me. Fond of children. If they don't talk. You don't talk. Look as if you wished to. Out with it! Don't be afraid."

" Oh, no! I 'm not afraid, now. Ought I to be? But, will you please tell me where you keep it? And why don't you wear it?"

" Eh? How? Keep it? Wear it? What?"

" Your cor'net. Suzan' says you can't be a real lord, 'n'ess you have one."

" Steenie!" reproved Mr. Calthorp, smiling in spite of himself.

" Good. Good. Let her alone. Hm-m. Coronet. Suzan' ought to know. Well. Did n't bring it."

" Oh!" In a tone of deep regret.

" No. Sorry now. If I 'd imagined disappointment — might. But — inconvenient. Don't wear it often."

" Oh," said Steenie again, surprised by the twinkle in the nobleman's eyes. " I did n't know. I s'posed you had to. But I should think it would be uncomf'table; 'cause gold is so heavy, and your head so smooth and shiny. I s'pose it would slip off."

His lordship's manners certainly were peculiar.

He nearly choked himself trying to suppress a laugh and to eat at the same time; but finally yielded to a real guffaw, as noisily as any cow-boy on the *hacienda.*

"Steenie!" said the manager once more, this time with real severity, and comprehending for the first time how sadly neglected the child had been.

But, fortunately, Lord Plunkett was very good-natured, and wisely divined that his small new acquaintance was rude ·from· ignorance, not intention. Dinner over, he made friends with her directly, and explained away the mistaken notions with which the housemaid had filled her head; while Steenie listened eagerly, delighted to find at last somebody who had both leisure and patience to answer "foolish questions."

Lord Plunkett did this without waste of words; and at the same time went poking about the place, enjoying the novelty of all he saw, and gaining from Steenie's talk a pretty fair idea of the daily life at San' Felisa. "Hm-m. So I see. Brought yourself up, my dear. No mother. Father busy. Servants ignorant. No church. No school. Well, well. Good thing for you, bad for me. Pity about his eyes. Bad, bad. Hope he won't be blind. Permanently."

"I hope so, too; though I don't know who you mean," said the little girl, sweetly.

"Good child. But — don't know? Why — father. Your father, of course. Hope he's the only one losing eyesight and going away. Hate new men. Old ones invaluable. Hope he'll get better. Come back. Bad country for eyes. Too much sunshine. Not enough green."

Steenie stopped short on the path. "What was that, sir, please? My — father — blind? My father — going away? Oh, dear Lordship, is that what you said?"

"Yes. Yes. Certainly. What? Not know it? Why else should I come? Hm-m. Queer. Starts in few days. Operation — maybe cure — "

But he did not finish his sentence; for the child had suddenly darted away from him, and to the side of the "tobacconist's sign," who was crossing the court at that moment. "Sutro! O my Sutro! My father is blind — and — going — away!"

"It is false!" cried the old Spaniard, with his ready and angry defiance of all things unpleasant.

"No, no — it is true! 'Cause the cor'net man said so!" And clinging to her ancient playfellow, Steenie buried her face in his blanket, and sobbed bitterly.

CHAPTER II.

KENTUCKY BOB.

THERE, she's found it out! And it's a deal worse than if her papa had told her first off!" said Suzan', at the kitchen door. "I never saw Miss Steenie cry about anything before, and I wish now that I'd a broke it to her myself."

"My, my! the poor lamb!" echoed Ellen, the cook, joining the house-maid. "No, she haint never been one fer cryin', — not even fer bumps er scratches. Sunshiny's what she's been, an' so I say. Does seem's if I could n't stay to cook fer no new manager's folks after that sweet angel. Good mind ter give notice myself."

"Oh, wait! Maybe it won't be so bad as we think. Master don't look blind."

2

"How can ye tell how he looks, 'hind them great goggles o' his'n? I guess it's bad as it can be, er he would n't give in to it. He's clear grit, an' so I say. That's where Miss Steenie gets her'n. See! she's spied her father comin' back from the valley! He rid away to call the boys together, 'cause his lordship wants to see 'em, I suppose. Well, he's right peart-lookin' yet; but man's born to troubles, an' he'll hev to take his share."

The women watched Steenie run with out-stretched arms to meet Mr. Calthorp; saw him check his horse suddenly, when he had almost ridden her down, and bend low to lift her to his saddle. They saw the child's arms clasp close about his neck, and fancied they could hear her wild outburst of grief. Then, with moistened eyes, but in true delicacy, they turned away from witnessing a child's first sorrow.

"Papa, is it true?"

"My darling, why do you cry? What true?" The well-trained horse stood still while the rider folded his little daughter close to his own heavy heart.

"About your eyes. Are you — blind?"

Mr. Calthorp shivered. Even to himself he could not yet acknowledge what seemed so plain to almost everybody else. "No, sweetheart, I am not blind — yet; but for a long, long time there has been something wrong with my eyes, and I dare put off no further the treatment which they require. So I wrote to Lord Plunkett and asked him to relieve me of my duties here, and I meant to tell you as soon as it seemed necessary. He came before I had expected that he could. He wishes to make a thorough examination of all Santa Felisa affairs, and to be fully informed concerning what has and has not been accomplished. I was glad, yet sorry, to see him; for our going away means leaving what has been my home for many years, and the only one you have ever known." He continued talking for some time, till he had given a very quiet and clear explanation, which soothed the excited child; besides, the words "not blind — yet" were quite enough to fill her buoyant heart with a hope that seemed certainty.

"Oh, how glad I am! And I s'pose the lordship did n't understand. I'm quite — quite sure he did n't mean to tell a wrong story, and I'm sorry I snatched my hand away from him. I'll go and 'xplain it now, if you will put me down, Papa, dear!"

Smiling, Mr. Calthorp complied; and chirruping to his horse, continued his course stableward, while Steenie sought the "cor'net man" to make her naïve apology.

"I guess I did n't behave very p'lite, Mr. Plunkett, but I hope you won't be angry; I don't like folks to be angry; but you see I did n't think of anything 'cept my father, — not then. And I want to 'xplain it, — he is n't blind — yet; and he's going to see a treatment; so he'll prob'ly get them fixed over all right. And if there's anything I can do to int'rest you I will; for I like you very much."

"Eh ? — So ? — Thank you. I like you, too. Bright — bonny — worth a fortune. Hm-m ! Better than coronets. Stick to it. Sit down ? Orange-tree, yonder. Now, then, talk."

Laughing at his mirthful manner and odd sentences, Steenie led her new friend to the seat he designated; and folding her hands in her lap, said politely: "I'll talk what more I know. T is n't much, I guess; only 'bout horses; I have n't told you 'bout them yet, have I ?"

"No. Horses? What? Whose? Go on."

"Oh, ours ! — No, yours, I s'pose they are. Maybe they're the 'boys.' We've trained them beautifully. Tomaso and Connecticut Jim both say it can't be beat. It's great fun !"

"Don't understand."

"No, I s'pose not. But — this way, like a 'circus,' my father says. They's thirty-three, all counted; and every man of us has tried to teach our horse something better 'n each other; and they're just too cunning for anything! Bob's kept the 'cup' for ever so long now; but I'm going to win it away from him some time, — see if I don't! Oh, I forgot!" The eager little face suddenly drooped at memory of that terrible "going away," which would be even earlier than the anticipated "some time."

"Why, why! — delightful! Never heard anything like it! See it, can I, — eh?" demanded his lordship, whose love for horses was very great.

"I hope — I s'pose so. I don't know. Kentucky Bob's the head of us. We all have to mind him; and sometimes he don't be very pleasant. But he's very nice and honest, my father says; and I love him dearly. Then we can't have a 'circus' till he gets over it again. My father says, too, it's 'cause he has a 'crank' in him somewhere. I s'pose that's what hurts him and makes him unpleasant. Don't you?"

"No doubt. Bad complaint; quite general; touch myself. No, don't go! All right to-day.

But — where's Kentucky Bob? Walk him out!
Won't refuse, — not me."

"No, I don't s'pose he would, on 'count of
your being a lordship. If you don't mind staying alone, I'll run and ask him. I saw him cross
the *arroyo* just a minute ago."

"Trot; but come back."

Steenie departed; and while she was gone
Mr. Calthorp walked gropingly toward the bench
where his employer sat. He could still see sufficiently to guide himself about, and his knowledge of places and voices aided him. His eyes
were screened by close-fitting goggles of dark
glass; but he had worn these so long that
Steenie had almost forgotten how he had ever
looked without them. Few men in his condition
would have held to his post as long as he had
done, nor was this course wise in him; but he
was not a rich man, and he had been anxious to
earn and save what he could for his little daughter's sake.

"Hm-m! Get around — first-rate. Little
girl's smart; like her."

"Thank you. She is, indeed, a brave, sunny
child. In some ways her leaving Santa Felisa
will be better for her. She should go to school
and mingle with women. Here she has no com-

pany but myself and the 'boys.' Old Sutro has devoted himself to her since her infancy, and loves her jealously. Indeed, they all love her; but that is not strange, for she loves them. Has she gone upon an errand for you?"

"Yes; Kentucky Bob. Circus; like to see it. Says maybe he won't; 'crank.'"

"Well — he is — very peculiar. However, he has a wonderful gift with horses; it seems almost like magic; and he has imparted much of his skill to Steenie. She is perfectly fearless. But I won't anticipate. Are they coming?"

"Yes. Hm-m! how old — she?"

"Ten years. I'll leave her to negotiate matters."

Steenie approached the orange-tree, leading by one hand a great fellow, whose face at that moment wore its most forbidding expression, and who seemed inclined to break away from his small guide; yet determined, in his own words, "to bluff her out." Catch him, a free-born American, truckling to anybody, even if that body were a genuine "lord," and, what was more, his own employer! He guessed he wasn't a going to get up no shows unless he wanted to! And he evidently did not so incline.

However, when he came quite near, and saw

the small, dumpy, red-faced old gentleman sitting beside Mr. Calthorp, his astonishment conquered every other sentiment. He a lord! Whe-ew! he might be anybody! and of no great account either. Plain suit of clothes, no rings, no watch-chain, no scarf-pin even; bald-headed, good-natured, sensible. As his observations reached this happy climax, Bob ceased tugging at his feminine guiding-string, and marched frankly forward. Her father could not see the action; but Steenie was amazed when the re-fractory ranchman doffed his hat and made a respectful, if somewhat awkward, bow. She had never witnessed such a concession before on his part.

"Good evenin,' sir; hope I see you well."

"Quite, thank you. Hear you're wonderful. Horses. Like to see, if suits."

"Well, sir, I'd like to 'blige; but, you see, it's against the rules. Once a week, an' no oftener, is what we agreed. No use o' rules if you don't stick to 'em. Exercise every Sunday; no other times in public. If I 'lowed the 'boys' to go it rash, say on odd days, they'd get the upper hand in no time; then where'd I be?"

From the tone of his voice, Mr. Calthorp judged that Bob "wanted coaxing;" but this was not his affair. From the moment of Lord Plunkett's arrival he had practically resigned all authority, so he did not interfere.

Now, my lord was, as has been said, very good-natured; but, like many other good-natured and unassuming people, opposition, or imposition, made him a little testy. Moreover, he was accustomed to command, not to sue; and he considered that he had already conceded as much as was necessary to this rough specimen of American manhood. His choler and color rose together; and he opened his lips with a very decided and undignified snort: " Woo-oo! Eh? Hey?"

But, fortunately for all parties, Steenie's bright eyes had telegraphed alarm to her loving heart; and with a quick little " 'Xcuse me!" she pulled Bob's surly face to the level of her lips, and whispered something in his ear.

Then, as if there had been a spring in his back, his head rebounded to the upright, his cheek actually paled beneath its tan, and he ejaculated fiercely, " Great — Huckleberries!"

It was the nearest approach to an oath which this strange man ever allowed himself; for, though he thought nothing of breaking the Sabbath by racing or gaming, he neither gave way to profanity nor indulged himself with a drop of spirituous liquor. He used to describe himself as "half marm, half pop;" and to attribute his sobriety and general uprightness to the "marm" side, all to the contrary, "pop." Years before, when, a hot-tempered lad, he had run away from "pop's" wrath, he had solemnly promised his weeping "marm" that he would "never drink nor swear;" and, to the honor of Kentucky Bob, be it said that he had loyally kept his word.

"Huckleberries! Little Un, you don't mean it! You would n't, would you?"

"I — I've got to, dear old Bob! But — there — there — there — I won't cry! I will not. And you 'll do it, won't you?"

"Well — I reckon! But — little missy — the boys won't believe it. An' — Say, Boss, is it true? Are you a goin' to light out?"

"Yes, Bob," answered Mr. Calthorp, sadly; "but from necessity, not choice."

"An' the Little Un — why must she go? Ain't nothin' the matter of her eyes, is they?"

"No, no; thank God!"

"Well, then; leave her here. We 'll take care of her. Square. Why — what — in huckleberries — 'll San' Felis' be 'ithout our little missy? Ain't she lived here ever sence she was borned? Ain't we be'n good to her? We 're rough, we be.

We ain't no lords, ner nothin' but jest cow-boys
er sech. But we're men. An' Americans. An' I
'low there ain't one of us but would fight till
he died fer the Little Un, afore harm should
tetch her. No! It must n't be. An' that's
square."

Even Mr. Calthorp, who had had abundant
proof, heretofore, of the "boys'" devotion to
Steenie, was surprised at the depth of feeling be-
trayed by Bob's words; for he could not fully
know all that the child had been to these men,
separated, as most of them were, from home and
its associations. Since the hour when they had
been permitted to carry or amuse her, a tiny baby
in long clothes, they had adopted her in their
hearts, each in his own way finding in the frank,
merry, friendly little creature an embodiment of
his own better nature. They had even, with the
superstition of their class, accepted her as their
"mascot," sincerely believing that every enter-
prise to which she lent her presence or approval
was sure to prosper.

To what other human being would Kentucky
Bob have imparted the secret of his wonderful
power over the equine race? Indeed, to none
other; and to her only because he loved her
so, and was so proud of her cleverness. And

now his big, honest heart ached with a new and bitter pain, as he faced the danger of her loss.

"Why, Robert! Why! Eh, what? Tut, tut. Good child. Understand. But — father. First claim. See?"

Angry Bob cast one scorching, contemptuous glance upon the nervous little lord ; and if looks could annihilate, the British peerage would then and there have been short one member. Stooping, he swung Steenie to his shoulder, and strode away toward the great group of out-buildings which made the home-piece of Santa Felisa rancho seem like a village in itself. In the thickest crowd of the employees who had been summoned to meet their newly-arrived employer he came to a sudden halt.

"Hello, Bob! What's up?"

"I — The — I wish to sizzle! Sho, I can't talk. Tell 'em, Little Un."

"Yes, Bob," answered Steenie, gently, patting the great head around which she clung for support. "But s'pose you put me down. I'm heavy. I'm such a big girl, now."

"No, you ain't. Hold you forever, if you'll stay."

"Stay? stay where?" asked somebody.

"Tell 'em," again commanded the Kentuckian; and waving her hand, she hushed them by this gesture to hear her words.

Yet, somehow, the words would n't come. For the second time that day the self-control of the child failed to respond to her needs. Her eyes roamed from face to face of those gathered about her, and there was not one on which she did not read an answering love for the great love she bore to it. Rough faces, most of them. Sun blackened, — sin blackened too, perhaps; but gentle, every one, toward her. Odd comrades for a little girl, and she a descendant of "one of the first families in Old Knollsboro;" still the only comrades she had ever known, and therefore she craved no other.

Twice she tried to speak, and felt a queer lump in her throat that choked her; and at last she dropped her face upon Bob's rough mane, her sunny curls mingling with it to hide the tears which hurt her pride to show.

An ominous growl ran round the assembly, and the sound was the tonic she needed. "Hmm! who's a makin' ther Little Un cry?"

"Nobody, boys! dear, dear boys! Not anybody at all! I'm not crying now; see?" Proudly her head was tossed back, and a determined smile

came to the still quivering lips, even while
the tears glistened on the long lashes. "You
see, it's this way. I did n't know it till this
very day that ever was, or I'd have told you.
'Cause I've always been square, have n't I?"

"You bet! Square's a brick!"

"But all the time my father's been getting
blinder an' blinder, an' I did n't even s'pect anything 'bout it. I thought he wore goggley things
'cause he liked 'em; but he did n't: it was 'cause
he had to. And now, if he don't go away quick,
he can't get his poor eyes fixed up at all. So he
is. He's going 'way, 'way off,—three thousand
miles, my father says, to a big city called New
York, where a lot of doctors live who don't do
anything but mend eyes. My grandmother lives
in a little town close to New York, and we're
going to her house to stay; and—and—that's
all. I have to do it, you see. I'm sorry, 'cause
I love you all; but he's my father, and I have
to love him the biggest, the best. And I hope
you don't mind."

"No, no, no! Three cheers for the 'boss'!"

Given with a will; and by the time the noise
had subsided, Steenie's smile had become as bright
as ever, and that without any effort of her will.

"Good enough! Thank you, dears! And now

we 'll have an extra circus, won't we ? I 'd like to
'blige Mr. Plunkett ; and besides, you know, I —
I sha' n't have you, nor the horses, nor any more
fun — in that old New York !"

"Hold on, Little Un! Where 's your grit ?"
asked Kentucky Bob, passing Steenie from his
shoulder to a convenient wagon-box.

His sudden change of tone astonished her.

" Hain't I allays fetched ye up to do the square
thing ? If your dooty calls you to N' York, — to
N' York you 'll have to go ; but, fer the honor o'
San' Felis', an' the credit o' your boys, do it colors
flyin' — head up — shoulders back — right face
— march !"

"I will, Bob ! I will ! I will !" cried Steenie,
impulsively. " You sha 'n't ever have to be ashamed
of your Little Un, and so I tell you !"

In the midst of the rousing cheers which followed, Lord Plunkett appeared. He could restrain
his curiosity no longer.

CHAPTER III.

SUTRO.

THERE was some suspicion among the other dwellers at Santa Felisa that Kentucky Bob had once been employed about a real circus, else how had he acquired that intimate knowledge of the "rules and regulations of the ring" which he so constantly quoted for their benefit or reproval?

Into this "ring" of theirs, the boxes, hurdles, and other such things which the riders had been accustomed to use were soon gathered, and the labor of arranging these gave a wholly pleasant diversion to their feelings. A card of invitation, beautifully engrossed by a vaquero who had passed from the halls of Harvard to the great solitudes of the Sierras, was issued to Lord Plunkett, and a seat of honor erected for him on the southern side of the campus, while a spreading canvas wall on the north was to serve as a screen for the preparatory operations of the various actors.

Needless to say, maybe, that having once been won over to the project of an "extra show," an enthusiastic determination was roused among the Santa Felisans to make this farewell entertainment of their beloved "mascot" eclipse everything which had ever gone before.

Nor did the interest end at this ranch; for mounted messengers were dispatched to invite the people of the neighboring estates to be present at the exhibition, and the invitations were as generally as promptly accepted.

But, of course, all this preparation took time to accomplish, so the hour had been appointed for one o'clock of the following day; and during the interval Steenie's thoughts were so full of the matter, her tongue so busy discussing it, that she neither felt the time long nor permitted others to do so.

Indeed, so affected was everybody by the pleasant excitement of "getting ready," that evening came before Lord Plunkett and his manager were finally seated with their books before them and a secretary at hand, to examine into the business which had brought them together. Even then his lordship would gladly have waived the matter, had he been allowed. "For ten years. No, twelve. Ship-shape. Paid well. Prompt. What more, eh? I'm satisfied. Why not you?"

"But, my lord, I cannot be. Any new manager will have enough to learn, even without all that I can do for him. It is a great responsibility; and, my lord, I would respectfully suggest that in the future you visit this part of your property oftener than once in a dozen years."

"Hm-m! maybe; don't know. Planned to stay a year now. Girl going away. Give it up. Consider. She comes back; so 'll I. Like her. Credit to you; so's the ranch." Then the nobleman looked up as Sutro entered, bringing the "new manager's" card. "Hello, Mexican! Well, where? Indigestion? Missed you. Say you've character? Born here? Eh? What?"

Sutro bowed profoundly, but a malicious grin overspread his wrinkled face. "*En verdad!* Thy Excellency honors his humble servant. Ten thousand thanks. But the señor stranger is arrived."

Mr. Calthorp rose and advanced carefully in the direction of the door, extending his hand toward the new-comer, whom he immediately presented to Lord Plunkett; and, while these gentlemen were exchanging civilities, he turned sharply upon old Vives, whom he could hear rustling about near him. "Where have you been so long, Sutro? We have not seen you since dinner. His lordship has inquired for you several times."

"*Si?* He does the least of his household too great respect," answered the Spaniard, with haughty accent.

"Come, come, Sutro, don't be foolish! It would be wiser of you to conciliate both him and the new 'boss.' They can easily turn you adrift, and you are an old man. From the tone of your voice, I judge that you are angry. That is senseless, and I am sorry. I wish to feel that one as fond of my little daughter as you are will be quite happy and comfortable when we are gone."

"I bow myself in obligation to thee, Señor Calthorp," responded the old Castilian, servilely. But his mood was neither servile nor happy; and, as the retiring manager turned once more toward his successor, he sought the cozy corner of the office which Steenie called her own, and where she sat by her pretty shaded lamp, sorting her picture-books.

"*Hola*, my Little Un! But I have put a thorn in his shirt, no? Trust old Sutro!"

"How? What do you mean? And surely I can trust you to do 'most anything hateful when you look such a way! What have you done now, Sutro Vives? Tell me that!"

"Hi, hi, hi! maybe no. *Si?* Dost thou wish to go from San' Felisa to the land of snow and ice and no sunshine? Answer thou me that!"

"You know I don't wish it; but I must, that is all. But, wait, how do you happen to know anything at all about it? You ran away directly after dinner, and now you've just come in!"

"Pouf! thinkest thou an old caballero knows nothing but what a baby tells him? I have known for — this — long — time all that has been planned for the little señ'rita. *Si! Lo dicho dicho* [what I have said I have said]."

For a moment Steenie was silent, unable to answer this argument. Then she cried triumphantly: "But you need not tell me that. A 'long time' may be from this very mid-day that ever was, but from no longer. Does anybody at San' Felis' ever tell Sutro Vives secrets? In verity, no; for Suzan says you are a sieve that holds nothing. At the *Natividad*, poor dear old caballero, with a word they don't want spoken? Why, nobody. And if you'd known about my father's eyes and all, you'd have told

me the very first minute! You would so, my
Sutro, you could n't have helped it!" clapping
her hands.

It was the señor's turn to look crestfallen.
What his little lady declared against him was
quite true; but this had never prevented his
adopting an air of great mystery and secrecy
whenever the slightest occasion offered. Poor
old Sutro Vives was not the only one in this
world bigger in his own estimation than in that
of anybody else.

But he rallied as swiftly as she had done.
"*Tente!* what of that? He will not stay at San'
Felisa — yes? In verity, no; I have taken care
about that."

"Sutro, you look, you truly do look, naughty!
What badness have you been doing now, señor?
Answer me that."

"Is the truth badness? Then have I been
bad," retorted the other, bridling. "I have told
him the truth, this not-wanted, unmannerly,
new director-manager. Thou belongest to us, —
to the vaqueros and caballéros, and everybody
who dwells at San' Felisa. It is in thee the
'good luck' lives; and thou wilt never be allowed
to go away from us, so I tell thee! There will
be mutiny, uprising; what Connecticut Jim calls

'strike.' But go from Santa Felisa, thou? No!
— a thousand times *no!*"

Unperceived by them, Lord Plunkett had for-
saken the other table and the business talk, which
he found tiresome, for that of the pair in the cozy
corner, which appeared to be interesting; and he
had thrown himself upon a lounge which the back
of Steenie's big chair hid from view, to play the
part of eavesdropper; only in this case it seemed
not ignoble, for the two animated disputants
spoke quite loudly enough to be heard by anybody in the room who had chosen to listen. He
had, therefore, enjoyed the whole dialogue, and
he now leaned forward to watch Steenie's bright
face and to catch her reply.

"But I answer you and Jim and everybody —
yes! Where my father goes I will go, and all
this silly talk won't stop me! Next Saturday
morning, Sutro Vives, the noisy black engine
will stop at San' Felisa station, and Papa Calthorp and I will get into one of those big cars,
and will go whizz, away, away! — where you nor
Bob nor Jim nor nobody can do wicked, hateful
things to the Little Un, never again!"

Wrought up by the pathos of her own picture,
Steenie's self-control gave way at this juncture,
and bounding toward her father, who seemed at

that moment to be a cruel enemy, and yet her only friend, she astonished him by a torrent of tears and embraces which effectually stopped all further conversation.

"Sutro!" called Mr. Calthorp, sternly.

"*Si*, señor; how can I serve thee?"

"Here, go with Miss Steenie and find Suzan'. Daughter, let me see no more of this childishness. Such rebellion is unworthy of you and most distressing to me. Good-night."

Poor Steenie! her tears ceased instantly, and her grief turned to anger. At that moment she felt that she had not a friend in the world, and her proud little heart resented the apparent want of sympathy she met with everywhere. With a very decided stamp of her little boot-heels, she marched out of the room, — "eyes front, right face," as Bob would have commanded, though not in a spirit to be commended.

"*Lastima es* [it is a pity], my Little Un!" cried old Sutro, hurrying after his darling, only to have her turn fiercely upon him, and order him to "keep his pity to himself. And I want no Suzan'! I want nobody, — nobody at all!"

Ten minutes later a very wet and heated little face was buried in the white pillows, and Steenie Calthorp had settled herself in bed, convinced

that she was the most ill-treated child in the
world, and resolved to enjoy her misery to the
utmost.   Only unfortunately for her doleful
plans, she was by nature very sunny and hopeful, and she was also perfectly healthy.   In about
two winks she happened to think of the next
day's "circus," and before she knew it she was
asleep, with a smile upon her lips.

Suzan' entered softly and stood by the bed for
a moment, shading her lamp with her hand and
lovingly regarding the little maid.   "Bless her
dear heart! she's shed more tears this day than
in all her little life before.   But she's happy
now, — happier 'n anybody else at San' Felisa.
My, my! what'll ever we do without the Little
Un?   But master, he's worried about her crying;
though, sure, if he'd bothered less about books
and business, and more about his own pretty flesh
and blood, maybe his eyes'd a been better the
now, poor man!"

Then she went away as gently as she had
come; and when next Steenie awoke, the brilliant California sunshine streaming in at her
window was not brighter than that within her
own heart.

"Such a day, such a day!   Will it ever come
noon!"

"True. And all too soon, Miss Steenie, for that I 've to do. Because, what has his lordship done but give orders for a big feed for all the people who are coming to see you show off?"

"To see — me, Suzan'? Why, not me, but all the boys. I 'm not to do a thing till the very last, Bob says; and then only just ride and drive a little. Maybe they will get tired, and won't stay till the end, so I won't get a chance to do anything; 'cause Bob says he 's 'ranged a dreadful long program. I think that 's what he called it."

"In verity, *querida* [my darling]! I believe you are the only one worth seeing. Lord Plunkett says. I heard one of the fellows giving him some talk about you, and he kept rubbing his fat little hands, and saying things so odd. Sounds like water coming out of a bottle. 'Wonderful!' 'Strange!' 'Hm-m!' 'What?' till I had to laugh. Think of — him — for a lord! Much I care to read stories about 'ristocratics any more! He has n't any 'raving locks,' nor 'coal black eyes,' nor nothing. Is n't half as handsome as a'most any of the boys."

"Well, well! Never mind him! Hurry up with my hair, won't you, please? My! how you do pull! I wish my father'd let me wear it short, like his; don't you?"

"*Caramba!* No. Your hair is the prettiest thing about you, except your eyes, and maybe — "

"Stuff! who cares for pretty? If I had to twist my hair up in rags every night, like you do, dear Suzan', I'd be mis'able. But I s'pose you can't help it. You're grown up. It must be dreadful to get grown up, and as old as you are, poor, nice Suzan'!"

"*Si?* Humph! And me only twenty-five my last birthday. If it was Ellen, now—"

"Never mind Ellen. And I love you, dear Suzan', if you are old; and I'm sorry ever' time I'm fidgety 'bout my hair. You won't 'member it against me, will you, after I'm gone? 'Cause I don't mean any badness; it's only this quick temper and can't-keep-stillness of mine. I just want to run, run, or something, all the time. And keeping tidy, like my father says, is a bother. There! you've done, have n't you? Can I go? Kiss me, Suzan'!"

Away danced Steenie, leaving her kind attendant feeling already heavy-hearted in anticipation of the time when there would be no restless little creature for her fond fingers to attire, and no little outbursts of impatience to correct.

But presently, all other thoughts save those connected with the immediate affairs of the day were banished by the tasks which Suzan' found to do. There were chickens to roast, cakes to bake, biscuits by the hundred to be made, and pies — such rows of pies! that the arms of cook Ellen and her assistants, Win Sing and Lun Hoy, ached with the rolling of pastry.

But they were not dismayed. Not they! Did n't they always cook just as much when the sheep were sheared, or the feast after the " round-up " was held? A pity if Santa Felisa could n't respond to any demand made upon her larder, — especially by order of her owner, a real live British lord!

So the great ovens were fired, both in the house-kitchen and in the old adobe cooking-sheds outside; and a corps of white-aproned helpers attended the roasting and stewing and baking of all the good things which Mistress Ellen and her aids prepared. While under the eucalyptus-trees bordering the arroyo, Suzan' gayly directed the spreading of the long tables that would seat, if need be, full two hundred guests.

" Oh, is n't it fun!" cried Steenie, darting about from one point to another of the gay and busy scene; and always having in tow the perspiring Lord Plunkett, who found no breath left for even his short sentences, but contented himself by

beaming graciously upon each and every one he
met.

"Tug an' a canawl-boat!" said Bob, regarding
the pair somewhat jealously. "Don't see why
the Little Un need stick to him so closet, even
if he is a bloated lord!"

"Never you mind, Bob! Let the Little Un
alone. Ain't she happy? Ain't she a purty sight?
Brim full o' smiles an' chipper as a wren? What
more do ye want?"

"Nothin'. But 'pears ter me she need n't be so
powerful glad 'bout leavin' us. I—don't feel much
like laughin'. And she 'd oughter be practisin'."

"Don't worrit. It 'll be all right. Little Un 's
square. She won't ferget us, you bet! An' she 'll
do the 'great act' all the better fer bein' light-
hearted. Land! I only hope them cold-blooded
Easterners 'll make her half as glad as she 's always be'n at San' Felis'! But — ain't it gittin'
nigh dinner-time? Folks air beginnin' ter come
a'ready. Understan' the spread, general, ain't
ter be till afterwards?"

"No. An' the one 't carries off first prize is ter
perside. Well, I hope it 'll be our 'Mascot.' Do
me prouder 'n if it was myself."

"Me, too," echoed his comrade, and departed
to snatch a hasty luncheon.

At the same moment, Lord Plunkett announced, breathlessly: "I—I can't. Stop. Wait. Hungry. As — a — grizzly. Ever since — I came. Beats everything. Appetite. Come. Eat."

"Oh, you dear, funny man! However can you think about eating — now? Why, I just want one o'clock to come so much I can't wait!"

"Eh? What? Not afraid? Ride — same's nobody here?"

"Why — yes," answered Steenie, slowly, as this new idea presented itself. "Why should n't I? Indeed, I ought to do a great, great deal better; 'cause I would n't like to dis'point dear old Bob. Nor you," she added politely.

"Hm-m. Bob first. Then — me. Hm-m. You 're no — Anglomaniac. See that. Plain."

"Wh-a-t, sir?" asked the little girl, astonished by the long, strange word he had used.

"No matter. Nice child. Spunky — but good. The way I like them. See here?" He held up a small purse in which were displayed six glittering double eagles. "Prizes. Eh? Win 'em? Highest — three; next — two; last — one."

But Steenie was a little California girl, and her eyes were not dazzled by the sight of gold. Of its intrinsic value she had no idea; for in the

course of her short life she had had no occasion to
use any money.   The prizes, therefore, repre-
sented nothing to her beyond themselves; and
as playthings she did not care for them.

"Are they?   Then I hope the boys will get
them all.   'Specially Jim.   He's got a mother,
an' she's got a consumption, or something.   And
he's going to bring her out to live in California,
sometime.   It's ter'ble cold where she stays now,
my father says; and he 'vises Jim to fetch her.
They're money; and they would help, would n't
they?"

"Hm-m.   Yes.   And you— don't want them?"

"If he can't win them I do.   I'd rather he'd
get them himself, 'cause he's so pleased when he
beats anybody; but if he can't — why, I will —
I hope.   Now I know 'bout them, he must have
them."

"Hm-m," said Lord Plunkett again, grimly.
"Oddest child.   Like her.   Immensely."

"Steenie!" called Mr. Calthorp; and she darted
toward him.   "Are you sure that you wish to
ride in this exhibition, darling?   Are you timid?
Because there are a great many here, it seems;
and you need not if you do not like.   It will be
different from an ordinary occasion."

"But I do wish, Papa dear, if you don't mind;

because Bob would break his heart if I did n't.
He told me so. And I 'm going to win, too.
Then I 'll get a lot of money to give poor old Jim,
for his mother. Yes, yes! I want to ride! And
I will — win! "

CHAPTER IV.

SUTRO'S EXHIBITION.

BEFORE the entertainment really began, Sutro Vives gave a little private exhibition on his own account; and his dashings to and fro across the arena, directly in Lord Plunkett's point of view, were intended to excite that gentleman's curiosity and admiration, — which object was accomplished.

"Gorgeous. Old Spaniard. Silver. Robbed a mine."

Steenie, mounted on her piebald Tito, was standing close to the seat erected for the proprietor, and explained for his benefit: "Oh, Sutro has had all those things for ever so long; since he was a young man, I b'lieve. He said he would show you what an 'old Ca'fornian caballero was like!' See! He's all red and yellow and white. Listen to the tinkle of the silver chains among his trappings! Isn't he proud as proud — my Sutro? My father says his vanity would be 'musing if it were n't so 'thetic."

"Pathetic, dear;" corrected Mr. Calthorp, guided by her voice to her side.

"Pathetic? Why?" demanded Lord Plunkett.

" Because although his family was once wealthy, almost beyond compute, this poor old fellow is reduced to live a dependent on the lands that were his fathers', now a stranger's. His shrivelled body in that gay attire is but a fitting type of his changed fortunes."

"Why! Pshaw! Hm-m," commented his lordship, uneasily, distressed, as he ever was, by thought of any other's unhappiness.

"But, Papa dear, is n't he always talking about his 'estate'? He says that he is richer still than anybody hereabout; and that if he wants money all he has to do is — something or other!"

"The case with most of us," laughed Mr. Calthorp. "But Sutro does still retain a small piece of property, — small as compared with his former · possessions, apparently as worthless as

4

the Mojave. It is the last spur of the mountain range on the east, there; and, from its peculiar summit — a gigantic rock cleft into three peaks — called Santa Trinidad. Can you see? Point it out, Steenie, please."

" Yes, yes. See. Barren. Worth nothing?"

"So I think. So others have thought; or worth so little that in any transfer of this *hacienda* [estate] no purchaser has been anxious to possess La Trinidad, even if it had been for sale. There are many ugly traditions concerning it; but the plain and existing fact is quite ugly enough for me. It is infested with rattlesnakes, its cloven crest being their especial home."

" Hm-m. Crime. Exterminate. Should be."

" They do not wander far afield ; but, should they become troublesome they would, doubtless, be exterminated. The Indians are their natural enemies — or friends; seeming to have no fear of them, yet killing them off in great numbers for the sake of their oil, which is sold at high prices."

" Try to buy it. Trinidad. Hm-m. How much to offer?"

" I cannot advise you ; for Sutro would fix its value at an absurdly enormous figure. Besides, there is no hope of his selling. Hark! Isn't that the signal for the 'Grand Entree'?"

The notes of a fifer, playing merrily, floated across the arena. It was the signal agreed upon, and the thirty-odd horsemen who were to participate in the tournament gathered hastily behind the canvas screen on the opposite side of the campus.

Now, as has been said, Steenie was not expected to ride until the closing part of the entertainment; and she might have remained by her father's side, a mere spectator of all the rest, had she so desired; but when, at the first notes of the musician's call, old Sutro plunged spur into Mazan"s flank and dashed forward to the meet, her excitement rose to the highest. She sit still and watch! — while Tito's dainty hoofs were dancing up and down, like feminine feet eager for the waltz! No, no! Not so, indeed! Away she flew, and the piebald horse followed the brown mare behind the canvas wall.

" Tra-la-la! Tra-la-la! Toot-a-toot!" Emerged the young Mexican fifer on his sturdy broncho; and though he was proud indeed of his position that day, he was but the preface to the story, — unnoticed and of small account.

Sutro Vives really led the cavalcade, having

been appointed to this honor because of his age, and perhaps of his assumption, — for he was not the one to lose the prestige a little swagger gives to a weak argument ; and, although he was a fine rider, there were many others finer, and Kentucky Bob's great gray horse was far ahead of pretty Mazan' for symmetry and graceful strength.

However, the latter person was quite willing to " play second fiddle so long 's the Little Un 's with me," and she had naturally guided Tito to the gray's side.

The other actors in the entertainment followed in single file, and even a captious critic would have been forced to admit that they made a magnificent appearance. The glossy sides, the waving manes and tails, the gay caparisons and the regular hoof-beats of the beautiful animals fitly accorded with that free bearing of the stalwart riders, which is native to those who dwell in wide spaces and under no roof but the sky.

Upon Lord Plunkett, to whom all this was new, the impression made by that scene was profound. It exceeded his highest expectations, and they had been great. It made him feel himself a bigger man — physically and mentally— to be served by such men as these, and his kindly heart warmed to the "Americans" then and there with a degree of respect and cordiality he had never before accorded them.

Then the marchings and countermarchings began, and Steenie with a childish caprice darted out of the ranks again and back to her father's side, to whom she eagerly described all that was going forward; already learning with the intuition of her tender heart to become "sight to the blind," and assuming toward him a motherly air which sat quaintly enough upon her merry face.

"Eh? What? Hm-m. Why?" queried the guest of honor, as, some time later, a prolonged shout rent the air; for he could see nothing especially fine about the half-dozen lads who now rode into the arena upon the backs of their rough-coated bronchos.

"The programme!" cried Steenie, determined that a paper prepared with such labor by one of her "boys" should be duly appreciated.

"Hm-m! 'Number Seven. Knife Act!' Well? What?"

"Watch and see, dear Mr. Plunkett! Look — look! It's better than telling."

"And something as difficult as rare," added Mr. Calthorp.

The performers of "Number Seven" rode

quietly to the centre of the field, where one
stooped to plunge into the soft earth a large
knife, burying the blade to the hilt. Then the
six horsemen wheeled and rode slowly back to
the starting-point, whence, at the fifer's signal,
they began a wild and wide circuit of the " ring,"
repeating this several times. Each repetition
brought them nearer to the centre ; and at last,
when they had attained their maddest, fleetest
pace, the contestants uttered a shout, and bore
down upon the projecting knife-handle. Each
rider leaned far out of his saddle, his brow almost
sweeping the ground, his eyes fixed upon one
object, and his jaws set firmly for their task.

" But — don't understand.   Eh ? "

" The knife ! the knife ! See ! Each has one
trial ; each seeks to be first. See how they
crowd ! To pull it out with his teeth — See !
See ! Ah ! Natan' ! Na—tan' ! " The child's
voice rose to a shrill cheer, which was caught
up and echoed again and again.

Natan', indeed, who with the knife-hilt still in
his teeth and the fierce-looking blade presented
to the view of the spectators, lifted his hat in
acknowledgment of the plaudits, and rode straight
toward his beloved " Mascot." Then he accomplished a second feat, scarcely less difficult than

the first; for still at break-neck speed he reached
Steenie's side, and, without touching the knife
with his hands, thrust it deftly through a gay
little cockade fixed to Tito's head-stall. Then
he rode off again at the same unbroken pace, and
the " Seventh Number " of the programme was
ended.

"Hark! the fifer again! That is my signal!"
exclaimed Steenie, and waving her hand, galloped away to join the "boys."

"Number Eight" was a trial of skill almost
as difficult as the "knife race" had been, and
consisted in lifting from the ground, while riding
at full speed, a handkerchief which had been
thrown there. Now, Steenie's childish arms
could not compete with those of grown men,
and to supplement their shortness she was to hold
the knife which Natan' had won, and catch up
the handkerchief on its point, — if she could!

" Of course, it is a foregone conclusion that she
will win," remarked some person near Mr. Calthorp. " Those fellows idolize that child, and
they won't half try to beat her."

" Beg pardon, but it will be a 'fair, square'
trial," corrected the manager, turning toward the
speaker. " Steenie would not ride if they had
not promised her that. She is determined to

win, and I think she will, but she will do so honestly. She is quicker of motion than the others, and has a judgment about distances which seems like instinct. Besides, she and Tito have grown up together, and he understands her like a second self."

" Hm-m. Not afraid ? Danger ? Thrown ? "

" No, my lord, I am not afraid. She never was thrown, and she began her riding in the first year of her life."

" Eh ? What ? Amazing ! ' California story ' ? "

The proud father laughed. " A ' California story,' certainly, but a true one. Those fellows adopted her from the outset. They fixed up a sort of box-saddle, cushioned and perfectly safe, and strapped it on Tito's back. He was but a colt then, and I would not have allowed it per-haps; but they persuaded Suzan' in my absence, and when I saw how it worked I did not object. That is how it began. To-day — it ends."

A sudden wave of regret swept over poor Mr. Calthorp's heart, and turning away from a spec-tacle his affliction prevented his witnessing, he sought the retirement of his own apartments. " My dear little girl ! How changed her life will be ! From this freedom, this queenship, into the restriction of a country town and the sub-

mission of a schoolroom. Best for her, doubtless, but — poor little Steenie!"

Meanwhile Steenie neither pitied nor even
thought of herself. Side by side with four other
competitors, the piebald Tito kept his own place,
and tossed his head in equine enjoyment of the
excitement, while his young mistress applauded
him softly, with that praise which was incitement
as well.

Round and round the course, till the child's
eyes glittered and her cheeks glowed at the shouts
of encouragement which reached her from every
point. "Go it, Little Un!" "Hurrah for the
'Mascot'!" "The Little Un'll win, you bet!"

Such admiration is not the best mental diet for
a young human being, perhaps, but it had not as
yet hurt Steenie; and this was probably the last
time that it would be hers. With a loyal recognition of the good-will expressed, she waved her
hand and laughed and nodded, and "rode her
level best."

"Don't ye let nobody better ye, Little Un, else
you'll break Bob's old heart!" warned that
worthy, himself urging the gray horse to its
utmost.

"Not I!" returned his pupil, and dashed ahead.

Evidently the contest was between these two,

who had outstripped the rest, and now crowded each other for the shortest line toward the fluttering bit of cambric on the path before them.

"Hurrah! Hurrah! Tito, my Tito! Now, now! *Vamos!* Quick — a spurt! Win — you must!"

Under the very nose of the gray, the little piebald darted, with his rider half-hanging from the saddle and the knife ready for action. Even Bob's well-trained animal swerved a little, — a trifle merely, but it cost his master the prize.

No perceptible halt, but a dip, a rise, and Tito was already half-way across the course again, his mistress rising in her saddle, and waving triumphantly above her head the shining knife with the handkerchief it had pierced clinging about the hilt.

If they had cheered before, the crowd went fairly wild at that. Old Sutro and Connecticut Jim, sworn enemies that they were, turned in their saddles and hugged each other. Lord Plunkett shouted and waved till he looked apoplectic; and the reiterated cheers, "Another for the Little Un!" "Another!" brought Mr. Calthorp from his darkened office once more, this time with a smile upon his lips.

But the hour grew late, and the assemblage hungry. There was, accordingly, no delay in

Waving triumphantly above her head the shining knife with the
handkerchief. — PAGE 58.

giving the last exhibition, which was Steenie's alone.

" The child — prodigy — must not leave. Like her; like her!" said Lord Plunkett again, as the manager approached.

" I am glad that you are pleased; but I think that you will enjoy this driving scene even more. There is no racing, no danger. If the horses are not out of training, their action is wonderfully fine and graceful. Does that shout mean her entrance ?"

" No. Horsemen. Single. Taking stations — regular intervals — around the track."

" Yes; I understand. They do that to watch the horses, for the child's sake. At the least intimation of any animal being fractious or out of accord with the rest, the nearest caballero rides up and sets the matter right. Usually a word of command will answer, but sometimes an outrider accompanies her for the whole distance, — an extra one, I mean, besides Bob, who always follows close behind Steenie; generally in silence, but ready with advice if it is needed. That second signal — is it she?"

" Yes. Pretty! pretty!"

In her little wagon, to which was attached a wide, curious whiffle-tree, Steenie emerged from the canvas gateway, driving a pair of matched bays. The fifer had stationed himself in the centre of the plain, with a drummer beside him; and if the music they there discoursed was not sweet, at least it was inspiriting, and rendered in good time. Best of all, it was the same that had been used in training the horses, and they recognized it at once, falling into step immediately and almost perfectly.

The tune of "Yankee Doodle" fits perfectly the stepping of a horse; besides which, it is patriotic, and Kentucky Bob was nothing if not American. To the tune of "Yankee Doodle," then, this "act" was given; and though Mr. Calthorp smilingly apologized that they had not chosen "God Save the Queen," the delighted Englishman "did n't mind in the least."

"What, what! another pair, eh? Hey?"

"Has she made the circuit once?"

"Yes. Four; drives four!"

Around the course again danced the horses, four abreast, and not a break in their paces from start to finish.

"You darlings! you have never done so well! Do you know that I am to drive you no more? And are you being just perfect and splendid for that?"

"Maybe it's 'cause they're afeard of the Britisher!" said a vaquero, teasingly. "No, no! it's because they love me. Now, you others, remember, — not one blunder!" This to the third pair which was being attached to the cart, these last in advance of the other four.

It really was wonderful, — so wonderful that not a sound was heard save the strains of the music and the unbroken "pat-pat" of those rhythmic hoof-beats. But when the fourth circuit was completed, and waving the soft reins which her childish hands seemed too small to hold, Steenie stood up in her wagon behind the eight now motionless horses, a cheer went forth that dwarfed all which had gone before, and that caused actual tears to dim the vision of happy Kentucky Bob.

"Ah, ha! my Little Un! you done me proud! I can gin up livin' now! There'll never be nothin' better 'n that sight fer these blamed watery eyes! Not a fail, not a break-step, not a nothin', but jest cl'ar bewitchments!"

"There you spoke. Nothing but a witch-bairn, yet the bonniest this earth ever saw!" chimed in the Scotch gardener.

"Are you glad, dear Bob?"

"Glad? I'm heart-broke! I—I—Oh, my Little Un! you would n't go fer to leave San' Felisy after this, would you?"

"Hark! the prizes! That queer little English-man 'll bust his b'iler soon if somebody don't pay heed to him! He's a dancin' a reg'lar jig over there to catch our 'tention. I 'low you'll have to be took to him, Miss Steenie!" cried Tony Miller.

"An' I'm the man 'at'll do it!" responded her proud instructor, as, swinging his small pupil to her accustomed place on his broad shoulder, he strode away toward Lord Plunkett's bench.

"Hm-m! Gives pleasure! Clever—wonder-ful! Prize—won it! Eh? What? Every-body?"

"Huckleberries! Won it—of—course! Knew she would!"

Stooping low, Steenie extended her hand ea-gerly for the purse outstretched toward her, and for a moment a revulsion of feeling swept over the donor's heart. For the sake of the reward, then? So mercenary, was she?

But she had no sooner received it, and mur-mured her hasty "Thank you," than she de-manded, "Jim! Jim! I want Jim!"

Ah! my lord had forgotten "Jim," and he

watched curiously as the shy fellow made his way through the crowd to Bob's side.

" Here, Jim! I 've won it. It 's all for you. For your consumption, — your mother's, I mean That is, I 'm going to give it to you if you 'll promise me one thing. You will, won't you, dear Jim ? "

" I — I — Miss Steenie — I don't understand."

" Please don't be stupid, Jim! Think. Did n't you tell me 'bout the dear old mother an' her consumption, an' how, if it was n't for your 'habits,' you 'd bring her out to California to live in the sunshine; but fast as you get your wages, away they go on your 'habits' ? Did n't you, Jim Sutton ? "

" Ye-es," shamefacedly.

" Well, you thought the Little Un did n't know what 'habits' were; but I asked my father, and he says your 'habits' make you drink bad liquor an' stuff, an' waste your earnings. You 're a good man, my father says, an' trustible, only for them. So now, you see, we 've got ahead of them for once ; and I want you to take this money and send to that cold place and bring that good old mother right away out here. Then you won't be lonesome when I 'm gone, and she 'll keep you out of ' habits,' like you said she could. Will you ? "

"Will I, Little Un? You bet! An'—an'—
I can't talk. Bob, you take it. You say sunthin'
fer me, — purty, like it orter be said. But —
Lord! — I can't — she ain't — no Little Un, no
'Mascot,' she ain't; she's a genooine — angel!"

And Steenie wondered why almost everybody
cried.

CHAPTER V.

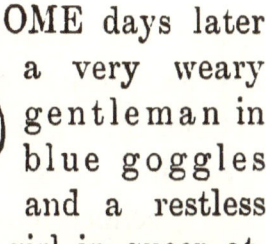

S OME days later a very weary gentleman in blue goggles and a restless little girl in queer attire, occupying a section of a railway sleeper, heard the welcome announcement of

MR. CALTHORP AND STEENIE

the guard passing through the train: "Next station will be Jersey City. Jer-sey-Ci-ty 's-the-next-sta-tion!"

Then followed the expressman with his insinuating question of, "Baggage, sir? Delivered any part of the city — baggage?" And the newsboy with his patois of, "N' Yo'k pape's? Pos'-Sun-'Elegram-World! Pape's? N' Yo'k pape's?"

By that time all the passengers were in a bustle of excitement, — women hunting and strapping stray parcels; men standing up to stretch their cramped limbs, while smiling congratulations to

one another that their three-thousand mile journey was safely accomplished.

Cries of, " Porter, my coat ! " " This way, Joe !
give me a brush next ! " " Oh, we 're almost in !
See ? " echoed here and there. Now, through rows
of houses, crowding faster and faster upon one
another ; and then over a net-work of iron rails,
between numberless cars of every sort, — constantly threatening a collision that was always
avoided, — pushed and panted the great " Over-
land," like an exhausted living creature longing
for rest.

All this was very familiar to Mr. Calthorp, but
quite new and formidable to his little daughter,
who nestled a bit closer to his side, and looked
about her with wide, observant eyes.

" Are you not glad, Steenie, my darling ? A few
more trifling changes to make, another two hours
of railway journeying, and then we shall be at Old
Knollsboro, at Grandmother's."

" As glad as anything, Papa dear, only — "
She checked herself suddenly, remembering her
farewell promise to Kentucky Bob that she
would " keep a stiff upper lip, an' not let the
' Boss ' see her weaken, no matter if she did get
homesick ! "

" Only what, dear ? "

" Why — why — I don't know. I feel so kind of queer and sick-y inside of me. I'm not ill — like eating too much candy; but — I don't feel very nice. I mean, it's all right, dear Papa. And I am really, truly glad. 'Cause then you'll get rested, won't you ? And you'll go to the eye-man and be fixed ; and then — maybe — I s'pose we'll go home again."

But already the train had stopped, and the porter, who had neglected these two for more importunate passengers, hurried up to give them a farewell " brush " and to help them with their parcels.

Alas ! poor Mr. Calthorp required assistance now as he had not done at familiar Santa Felisa. The close confinement, the almost sleepless nights of the long journey, and the growing anxiety, had affected his dim vision most unfavorably ; and the constant attention of his little daughter was necessary to him as he stepped from the car and joined the throng of liberated passengers passing forward into the station.

" Lead me into the ticket office. Can you make it out ? Ask any man in uniform."

Steenie looked up startled. There was a sharp, imperious note in her father's voice which was new to her, forced from him by the sudden conviction that he was no longer losing his sight, but that it was already lost, and that he had come eastward — too late.

Obediently the little girl touched the arm of an official, passing at that moment. " Please, sir, will you tell us where to go ?   My father — "

Mr. Calthorp took the explanation from her lips, and the man in the blue uniform looked compassionately upon these two who seemed so helpless, and whose manner so plainly bore the stamp of the far west, where threading narrow streets and dodging crowds are not every-day events.

" Sorry, little one, but — I 'm in a hurry.   Call somebody else ; " and he turned away.

As he did so, he caught the quiver of a girlish, travel-soiled lip, and a look of terror in a pair of big blue eyes ; and his feet refused to carry him further from the spot.

"Pshaw ! Almost train-time — hm-m. All right, Sissy.   Here, this way, sir ; " and slipping his arm through Mr. Calthorp's, the conductor of an out-going " express " wheeled sharply about, and guided his charges into a waiting-room, where he consigned them to : " Here, you, twenty-seven ! Look out for these folks ! There you are, little one.   This man will — "   The rest was lost in the distance as, with the skill of a veteran railroader,

the kind conductor boarded an already moving
car and disappeared.

A little act; but it cleared the mists from
Steenie's eyes and the anxiety from her heart,
for already "Twenty-seven" was saying in tones
of cheery friendliness, "All right, little missy!
Whar yo' an' yo' pa wanter go at?"

Mr. Calthorp's explanations were repeated with
such clearness that, in another moment, a cab had
been summoned, the travellers assisted into it, and
the station-man dismissed, with a smile shining
on his black face and a new quarter in his palm.

"I'm not a bit afraid now, Papa darling. I was
just at first, 'cause I did n't understand the place.
But don't you be worried now, we're all right;
and won't my grandmother be glad to see you!"

The returning invalid had his own opinion on
that matter; but he did not dampen Steenie's
courage by expressing it.

She went on, heedless of his silence. "My!
what folks and folks! More than ever came to
our circus — even that last one! And what
makes 'em almost run? They 'bout hit each
other, don't they? What big wagons! Oh, that's
a pretty horse! What big ones at that wagon full
of 'normousest barrels! Why are they so many,
many folks, Papa dear? Ah, we're stopping!"

More confusion — more changes; but always somebody at hand to guide them, for Mr. Calthorp had recovered his usual calm, alert manner, and could direct, if he could not see his path. A second brief railway trip, through which Steenie slept comfortably against her father's arm, and then — they were standing before the great door of a big white house, whence a brass lion's-head knocker grinned maliciously upon them. Though unguided by his eyes, Mr. Calthorp's hand rose naturally till it seized a curious bar-like tongue which hung from the beast's mouth, and struck it sharply against the polished plate.

"Whack! Rat-a-tat!"

Which brought the sound of approaching feet; and the door opened noiselessly, to show within the aperture a very stiff old man.

"Is Madam Calthorp at home?"

"Yes. But — my-soul-I-declare! Is it you, Mr. Daniel?"

"And you, Resolved Tubbs? I know your voice!" The visitor's hand was extended and clasped, though cautiously, by the trembling one of the old servitor. "My eyes —"

"I see, I see, sir. This way — you know — Madam is in the library. I don't think she expected you so soon."

" Maybe not. Though my secretary wrote."

" This way, sir." Mr. Tubbs had become himself again : a wooden-visaged old man who liked to express no opinion whatever, till it had been formed for him by his mistress of many years. He had not been able yet to judge whether that mistress would rejoice at this home-coming of her only son, or not ; and he waited his cue before knowing his own sentiments.

" Ah ! if it is as it used to be, I can find my own way, Resolved. The table by the wall — I recall its red wool cover with the black stamp exactly in the middle ; the two oaken chairs here ; and here — the hat-rack ! At home, indeed ! Even the very aroma of lavender and southernwood from those upper chambers is unchanged ! "

Then the blue goggles could not hide the gladness which leaped to the son's face as he turned the brass knob of the library door, and cried out, " Mother ! are you here ? "

There was a moment's hesitation, which Daniel Calthorp's dim eyes could not see ; then the rustle of silken skirts, and the stately old lady of the mansion had risen from her chair and crossed the room, to take her boy's hands in her own, and to imprint upon his bearded cheek a kiss of greeting. "So soon, Daniel? I had not looked for you until next week."

"Yes; I had a message sent. You see, I was able to get through a bit earlier, and I could endure no unnecessary delay. Here, darling, this is Grandmother."

In all her life Steenie had never looked upon the face of any woman who bore a kinship to herself, and the dreams of her romantic little heart had clustered about this unknown relative with an intensity such as only childhood knows. So she scarcely waited to have her elders' hands unclasped before she sprang forward between her father and his mother, and precipitated herself upon that lady's neck. "Oh, I thought you would be pretty! but you're prettier than anything I ever saw!"

Madam Calthorp staggered a little, — perhaps from the violence of this attack upon her person, perhaps from surprise at the words; then she quietly loosened the child's clinging arms and released herself. "You are an impulsive little girl, Steenie! Let me see, how old are you?"

"Ten; going on 'leven."

"Say 'eleven.' You are very large of your age; I should think you might be older."

Then there was an awkward silence, which the

son broke by groping across the room to a sofa in the bay-window, where he sank down as if exhausted. Steenie bounded to his side, flashing a defiant glance at the tall old madam as she passed. "What is it, my Papa? Are you ill?"

"No, no; not at all! But we are both travel-soiled, and unfit for your dainty rooms, Mother. What quarters have you given us? We will go and freshen up a bit."

Old Tubbs, still waiting outside the door, listened critically for his mistress's reply. From it he would form his own basis of action.

"I gave you the spare chamber, Daniel; your daughter can take the little room next." But Madam's voice, saying this, sounded as if she were somewhat perplexed.

"Hm-m!" said Resolved to himself, "if she'd answered up quick, 'Your old room,' I'd a knowed she was glad, an' meant things as they uset ter be. But — 'spare room!' that means he's comp'ny. She hain't fergot how he went away, ner the dozen years between. Well, my — soul — I — declare — I'm sure I know which side my bread's buttered! An' comp'ny it is!"

"Shall I carry yer bag, Mr. Daniel?" asked this astute servant, as the travellers emerged from the library.

"No; oh, no! thank you. I fancy I'm better able than you, old fellow. Nothing wrong with me but my eyes. This way, sweetheart."

Whatever the feeling of disappointment in Daniel Calthorp's heart, there was nothing but gayety in Steenie's, as she tripped merrily up the broad stairs behind him, — stopping now to examine the slender polished rods which held the carpet in place, and now to gaze through the window on the landing at the old-fashioned garden, where the late April snows still lingered in the clefts of the lilac branches and made a white border for the rows of box.

"Oh! is n't it just like a story-book? And my grandmother looks like pictures of queens. She makes me think of the cleanest things I ever saw. Did you notice?"

"Be eyes for me, little one, and tell me just what you saw. Her face, is it wrinkled? Is her hair gray? Did she wear glasses?"

"Her face is white, — whiter than anybody's I ever saw, 'cept Irish Kate's little baby's. And her hair is like that pretty snow out there, all round little rolls each side her eyes; and she has some soft white stuff on her head, and more around her neck and her wrists. Her dress is black silk, and — I love her!"

"I'm glad — very glad of that!" exclaimed Mr. Calthorp, earnestly. The power of Steenie's love he believed to be irresistible.

"But is n't Mr. Tubbs funny? He makes me think of raisin grapes that have n't dried right. And he wears his spectacles up on the bald part of his head; and he looks lots older'n Sutro. How old is he, Papa?"

"Maybe seventy; I don't know exactly. Now, can you make yourself tidy alone? There are no young women servants in this old house, and you must do everything you can for yourself. But I will help you with your hair if it bothers you, as I did, or tried to do, on the train."

However, he was saved this trouble; for at that moment came a knock upon the door of the little room assigned to Steenie, and, at her swift opening of it, an old lady entered.

At least Steenie called her "lady," and was amazed when this prim person, in the black alpaca gown and wearing spectacles, remarked: "Madam sent me to wash and dress you. Come here!"

"But — I — I can do it for myself. I'd rather. I'm very soiled; the car was so dusty. And you look so clean! Everybody is so ter'ble clean here!"

"Hoity-toity! Come. I've no time ter waste."

Steenie moved forward, slowly, and greatly wondering. It had seemed all right to have gay young Suzan' preside at her toilet, but a severe-looking and venerable creature like this was quite a different matter.

"Where is the bath-room, please?"

"The bath-room! There ain't none. Hm-m. Did ye expect a palace?"

"A palace! I was talking 'bout water. What'll I do then? I've been a'most a week in that dirty car — and I — Maybe Papa knows." She applied at her father's key-hole for advice, and he took the direction of affairs into his own hands.

"Just fix up a tub in your old wash-room, won't you, Mary Jane? And let Steenie have her splash there. It will save messing your clean room, and I will explain to my mother."

Mary Jane went away with a sniff, and her nose in the air; sternly muttering about "folks turning the house topsy-turvy, an' thinkin' the hull world b'longed to 'em;" and Steenie followed, meekly. She was very much in terror of the sharp-visaged old spinster, whose favor she had, however, unwittingly won by her desire for cleanliness; although Mary Jane was not the woman to admit that at once. She was shown into the bare-floored, and rather chilly wash-room, where a round blue tub was deposited upon the boards with a decided bang, and promptly partially filled with several bucketsful of cold water from the "system" pump, after which Mary Jane disappeared.

Then the new-comer forgot her fear in her curiosity, and was busily poking about, inspecting her surroundings, when her ancient attendant re-entered, tossed another pail of boiling water into the previous ones of cold, and again withdrew.

An hour later, Steenie, very fresh and dainty in her white frock, and with her rebellious curls brushed into a semblance of order by her father's untrained hand, bounded gayly through the long, cold halls, and in at the library door, just in time to overhear the old servant explaining to Madam: "She'll be a cruel lot o' trouble, an' mebbe the death on us with her noise; but — she's clean! Why, ma'am, she says she takes a hull body-wash, ever' day on her life, an' some-times twicet! An' if it's the truth, she's one youngun out of a million! an' the only one't I ever see't liked water in her nateral state. She's a phenomely. But — my floor! When I went in, half an hour arterwards, there she stood,

dancin' a reg'lar jig, roun' an' roun', an' splashin'
the suds all over her an' the boards, an' ever'
conceivable thing! I scairt her out, lively; an'
all she could say fer herself was: 'It seemed so
good an' funny to use a roun' tub, stidder a reg'-
lar long one.' She'd a splotched out the last
drop in another minute. She must a be'n brung
up a reg'lar heathen, an' her Mr. Dan'l's only!'"

Steenie, poised on tip-toe, listened to the close
of the harangue; certain from the words that
Mary Jane was frightfully angry and from the
tone that she was rather pleased. But, at that
moment, Madam Calthorp perceived her, and mo-
tioned silence to the speaker.

"But I'm not a heathen, Mary Jane! My
father says a heathen is one who worships idols,
an' I would n't be such a dunce as that. I've a
whole lot of Indian idols at San' Felisa, an'
they're as ugly as ugly. The silly things make
them out of the same clay they do their jars and
dishes, an' the jars are far prettier. My father
says —"

"Steenie, why have you put on a white frock
on such a day as this?"

"Why?" repeated the puzzled visitor. "It's
a clean one, only wrinkled in the packing."

"But — a white dress in April! It is wholly

out of place. You will get sick, and have to be taken care of. Take it off at once."

All the gayety died out of the child's face, rosy from recent scrubbings with soap and water, and radiant with health, and a look of strange perplexity succeeded. "I — I can't, Grandmother. I have n't any other."

" No — other — frock ! "

"Not that is clean. My car one is ter'ble dirty an' dusty. My father says it is n't fit to wear any more; and my horse-back one is n't unpacked; an' my rest are just like this. I 'm sorry if it is n't right ; " with a deprecatory little gesture that appealed strangely to Madam Calthorp's cold heart.

" Well, well! Do you wear such clothes as these all winter in California ? "

" Yes ; I do. My father says 'at white is the only 'propriate color for a little girl."

" White is not a color, Steenie. Learn to be accurate. But — go and ask Mary Jane to give you my gray cashmere shawl, then put it on directly. If you have no suitable clothes, some must be procured for you."

" Yes 'm," answered Steenie, obediently, and ran away, — to return presently, sheathed in a great gray calyx, from which her flower-like face peered mischievously out. Then her father's steps were heard descending the stairs, slowly, and the child darted off, once more, to clasp his arm with a vigor that denoted deep emotion. "Oh, Papa, it was too bad we came! Do you know she does n't want us? My pretty, very own Grandmother! She does n't say so, but I know it. She does n't!"

Daniel Calthorp drew his darling closer to his side; and though he smiled brightly enough, his own heart echoed the disappointed words. He had known from the moment when his mother's voice had fallen on his now super-sensitive ear that his coming had brought her no pleasure, and that she had been too truthful to put into her welcome a warmth which she did not feel.

"Then we must be so patient and kind to her, sweetheart, that she can't help being glad, after awhile. I depend upon you, my Blue Eyes, to work a miracle."

So they entered the Madam's presence once more, and together; and though she saw something pathetic in the grouping of that helpless pair, the disturbance and annoyance which their coming was to her calm, self-sufficient life far outweighed her pity.

CHAPTER VI.

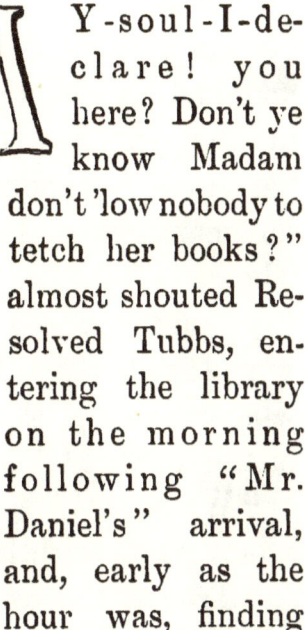

M Y-soul-I-de-clare! you here? Don't ye know Madam don't 'low nobody to tetch her books?" almost shouted Resolved Tubbs, entering the library on the morning following "Mr. Daniel's" arrival, and, early as the hour was, finding

STEENIE READING.

the place already occupied by Steenie. Sprawling flat upon the hearth-rug, and supporting herself upon her elbows, she turned the leaves of a richly illustrated folio, while piles of other volumes were heaped about her, in careless disregard of injured bindings. She did not heed, because she did not hear, the reproof; for at that moment her childish soul was deep in the

"Inferno," following the poet's dark imagings by the aid of Doré's darker pencillings. She had had the handling of few books in her short life, but she "took to them" as naturally as did her stately grandmother, whose quiet existence for many years had been among them almost wholly.

"Don't you hear, sissy? You must n't tetch 'em, I tell ye! Git up, quick! I — I dunno what on airth she 'd say if she was ter come in this minute!"

"What, sir?" asked Steenie, absently, lifting a face white with horror, "is it true?"

"True as the gospel; you 'd better look out!"

"Is it near here, — near this very Old Knollsboro' town?"

"Hm-m! I vum I never see nothin' like ye! I do b'lieve ye ain't right bright!"

"Is it?" again demanded the child, oblivious to any personal remarks.

"I dunno nothin' 'bout printed trash, an' you hain't no call to, nuther. But you 'll hear sunthin' 'at 'll make yer ears buzz if you don't put them books right square back where ye got 'em! I ain't a goin' ter wait on ye, like you 'pear ter be uset ter havin' folks do! I 've got the fires ter 'tend, the chores ter do, an' ten thousan' more

pesky things, all this very mornin', an' my lumbago achin' me fit ter split."

"What's a lumbago?" asked Steenie, sitting
up cross-legged, and trying to hold the great book
on her small lap.

"It's — Thunder an' lightnin'!   Ou — uch!"
With a groan that was almost a yell, Resolved
arose from the stooping posture which, in an
unwary moment, he had assumed before the grate
he was cleaning, and clapped his gnarled fingers
to "the small of his back."

Whereupon Steenie likewise sprang up and
retreated to the further corner of the apartment, leaving the volume *de luxe* to fall where
it happened.   "What's the matter?" she demanded, from that safe distance, half-laughing,
half-crying, for her vivid imagination had been
overwrought by the lurid pictures she had been
studying, and Mr. Tubbs's shriek seemed to pres-
age some of the intolerable torments which she
had seen depicted.

"The lumbago, I told ye!   Blast a youngun,
— etarnally askin' questions!   Wait till ye git
ter be as old as I be, an' you'll know, I guess!"

"I'll wait!" responded Steenie, willingly, and
with no intentional disrespect.

"Ye will, will ye? you saas-box!   Where ye

ever lived ter have no respect fer age?" And, mindless of his affliction, the exasperated Mr. Tubbs started in pursuit of the offender, to drive her from his sight.

But she, mistaking his intention, and fancying a terrible resemblance between his pain-contorted face and the anguished ones of the "Inferno" engravings, crouched back in her corner, and, throwing her arms up rigidly above her head, uttered shriek after shriek of terror. Beyond her mild dread of "seeing folks angry," it was her first experience of fear, and it took absolute possession of her mind.

"Shet up! shet up! My-soul-I-declare, you're the beatenest youngun I ever see! Why on airth could n't ye stay back thar in Californy stidder comin' ter torment them 'at don't want ye?" But as, in his eagerness to quiet this unprecedented disturbance of that orderly house, the deluded servant continued to advance menacingly, Steenie continued to scream; until, in the midst of the uproar, a white-haired figure appeared in the doorway, when she darted instantly forward and buried her face in her grandmother's skirt.

As Resolved afterwards expressed it, he "was struck dumberfoun' an' could n't say nothin';"

and as Steenie was also speechless, the startled mistress of the house was left to draw her own conclusions from the scene.

"Steenie, look up!"

Steenie shivered and obeyed. "Is it true, Grandmother? Does he really, truly know?" Again that unwonted stirring in the hitherto cold heart of the Madam moved her to ask almost gently, "What true, child?"

"About men being twisted into trees — and swimming in flames — and — and — awful everythings! He says so."

The lady's eyes strayed more critically over the apartment, and, if any of that perfectly trained woman's movements could ever be such, the start she gave was violent. Steenie felt herself pushed suddenly aside, and saw her grandmother cross hastily to the ill-used Dante, which she raised with a care far more loving than she had yet bestowed upon the motherless child of her blind, only son.

"Steenie! Steenie Calthorp! Listen to me. Understand me — fully. I forbid you ever touching a single volume in this room, in this house, which I do not, personally, place in your hands."

The little girl was too surprised to speak.

When, at last, she found her voice, she asked, innocently enough: "Are n't they to read? The books!"

"By those who comprehend their value. But you are to obey me, implicitly. Will you?"

"Yes 'm. So my father said," answered Steenie, sweetly. "But, you see, I did n't know they were n't to be looked at till Mr. Resolved said so. We did n't have any books at San' Felisa, 'cept Papa's figurey ones, and some 'at did n't have pictures. Only mine. The 'boys' used to bring me lovely books, ever' time they went to town. They was 'Jack the Giant Killer,' and the Andersen man's, an' a beau-u-tiful 'Mother Goose'! Father Antonio sent me a prayer-book; but it was all in Latin, and my father says I must learn English first." The presence of her grandmother had reassured the child against any danger from the lumbago-frenzied Mr. Tubbs, and she now leaned contentedly against the wall, coolly watching the disarranged volumes being returned to their shelves, and quite free from any anger against anybody. But she could not forget what she had seen, and when Madam Calthorp had finished her labor, had closed and locked the glass doors of the old-fashioned book-cases, and turned to leave the room, she went forward and clasped the lady's hand. "Did you ever read that book, Grandmother?"

"Yes."

"Is it English?"

"No, Italian. Dante, who wrote it, was an Italian poet."

"Is it near here,— where those poor people are?"

"Steenie! Ah, how can I tell!"

"Can't you? I thought you knew everything. My father says you are the most intelligy woman of his 'quaintance. He said he wished I could be like you; but he did n't think I could, 'cause something was the matter with my nature, 'at made it diff'rent."

"Say 'dif-fer-ent,' Steenie. Speak all your words distinctly."

"Dif-fer-ent. It takes longer, does n't it?"

"It commonly takes longer to do things well than ill. It is the fault of the present generation to slur everything, in its rush for 'time.'"

"Yes 'm," assented Steenie, politely, to whom this was as Greek.

"Did you ever go to school, my dear?"

"No. But my father says I may while I 'm here. I don't much care about it."

"Why not?"

"Oh, 'cause. One thing, it's in a house, he says, an' I like out-doors. I never stay in the house, 'cept nights. Here comes Papa! Is breakfast ready? I'm awful hungry."

Steenie's manners and speech continually jarred upon Madam Calthorp's ideas of propriety; and propriety was the rule of her solitary life But, although she had dreaded this invasion of her quiet by a " noisy child," and by the son whose many years of absence had made him seem a stranger to her, yet she was impartial enough to acknowledge that there was something very winning and lovable about the little girl.

Breakfast over, mother and son retired to the library to " talk business," and the other member of the family party was left free to amuse herself as she chose. " Only take care not to meddle, nor get into mischief, darling," added Mr. Calthorp to his kiss of dismissal.

"Not if I can help it, Papa dear, but 'most ever'thing here seems to be 'mischief.' I think I'll go out-doors."

Madam did not hear this decision, or she would have forbidden it, — not from any desire to thwart Steenie's enjoyment, but because the child was not fitly apparelled to appear on the streets of respectable Old Knollsboro, where, though fashions were not advanced, very rigid notions were held of what should or should not be worn.

Bare-headed and in her white frock, still bundled about with the gray cashmere shawl, the little stranger wandered out into the garden, and thence to the street.

April was half gone, and till then the weather had been cold; but that morning came one of those sudden changes which seem like summer warmth gone astray. The snow-patches melted swiftly, the frozen sidewalks thawed, and the whole earth became a bed of softest mud, over which Steenie pursued her sticky way, too intent upon her other surroundings to notice what went on beneath her feet.

"How the birds sing! There are more birds here than at San' Felisa, I do b'lieve. And the sun shines a'most as bright. Dear me! I wish I'd worn my hat — but never mind. This shawl's awful hot. I'll take it off an' lay it on the fence. Hm-m. How funny! Everybody has a big white house an' a little white railing around it, an' that's all. But it looks pleasant down that road. I wish Tito was here. Dear, darling Tito! It seems —"

"Whooa! Whooa! I say! Hold — on — don't — whooa-a!"

Steenie turned swiftly round. Down the street

behind her galloped a wildly excited horse, with
a little girl on his back; while following fast
came a second beast, ridden by a terrified groom.
The small equestrian had lost her control of her animal, — if control she had ever had, — and he had
taken fright or become suddenly vicious; keeping
just so far in advance of the pursuer as to avoid
capture, and dancing upon his hind legs between
whiles, in a manner inimical to any rider's safety
and doubly dangerous to one so young as she who
still clung to her saddle, her fingers clasping the
pommel in the rigidity of fear.

"Oh, he's running away! The naughty
fellow!"

Thought and action came together; for the very
sound of a horse's foot-fall had roused Steenie's
spirit to its full activity, even before she had
turned to learn that the sound meant danger.

"*Hola! Hola!*" she cried softly, and bounded
into the road; skimming the muddy surface like
a swallow and racing as her old Indian friend,
Wanka, had taught her in the games at Santa
Felisa. She had thrown up her hand, warningly,
to the groom, who, aghast at seeing a second
child rush into peril, checked his own horse,
almost unconsciously.

"That's the wisest thing he could do! Why

did n't he stop before?" thought Steenie; "that
little girl's horse knew he was being chased,
and —"

The small hands on the pommel were slowly
slipping loose; but the fleet-footed westerner had
gained the gray beast's side, had sprung upon it,
had thrown herself astride the quivering shoulders,
and caught up the dangling bridle.

"Hold on to me, girl! Tight — my waist —
I 'll take care — *Hola, hola,* my pretty one! *Ce,
ce, ce!* Wouldst thou? But, no!"

How was it done? That is Steenie's secret,
learned from Kentucky Bob and loyally kept because of her promise; but this is what happened:
she leaned her face far forward till her pretty
lips were close beside the frantic animal's ear,
and there cooed to him in half-whispered sounds,
till he paused for one second to listen, — and in
that brief instant yielded his equine will to her
human one.

"Good boy! So, so, my hero! Softly now, — as
a well-bred horse should go! Don't you be afraid,
little girl! He 's — what 's his name?"

"Ki-inks," faltered a timid voice.

"Well, I should think so! He 's full of kinks;
but he 's a beauty! Are n't you, dear?" which
flattery the mettlesome creature seemed to heed,

for he fell into a measured pace, and tossed his mane proudly, as who should say: " Behold me! A fine fellow am I!"

A few rods further of this movement, then Steenie checked Kinks entirely; and though he quivered and trembled, and looked nervously around at the groom riding up and the crowds who had collected on the sidewalk, he suffered the restraint imposed upon him by the stroking of her soft little hands and her caressing voice. Then she asked: " Where do you live, girl? Do you want to go home?"

" Yes, yes! I live down there," answered the rescued child, loosing one arm from her preserver's waist sufficiently to point forwards down the avenue.

" Shall I get off? Can you ride alone?"

" No — no —no! Let me down! Please!"

" Wait. Let me tell you. Is he your horse?"

" Yes."

" Do you love him?"

" Not — now. I did — but now I hate him! Let me down!"

The groom approached and dismounted to obey this demand; but Steenie wheeled sidewise, so that Kinks could look his stable-mate squarely in the face.

"Not yet, little girl. He's beautiful, and you ought to want to ride him. Why don't you?"

"I'm afraid."

"You need n't be. Something made him angry; then he ran away. He 's ashamed now."

"Ashamed? Why, how do you know?"

"He says so, plain enough. See here, Kinksey, hold up your head. Look at your little lady an' tell her you 're sorry."

To the astonishment of every on-looker the little bareheaded stranger coolly seized the gray's forelock and pulled his head backward, so that his eyes could be seen ; and laughing softly, but lovingly, she maintained his position till his owner leaned forward and satisfied her own curiosity.

"Why — it is so! He does look as if he wanted to hide!"

It was quite true. If ever an equine countenance expressed shame and regret, that of the now humbled Kinks did so at that moment.

Probably it was the first time in their lives that the people in that wondering crowd had ever thought whether a horse was capable of facial expression ; and it gave them food for reflection. Either their own eyes deceived them, or the stranger child was a "witch," or — a horse did have emotions, — and showed them.

"Now, you won't be naughty and unkind to him, will you, — just because he did n't behave p'lite for once ? "

" I — I 'm not naughty. He 's nothing but a horse, and I 'm folks. I know things."

" So does he. He knows more 'n you or I do ; an' he did n't have to go to school, neither."

" You 're an awful funny girl."

" So are you. Say, shall I get off? Will you ride him alone ? "

" No — no ! Stay on. If you will, I won't get off at all. I 'll ride all the way home. Will you ? "

" May I ? '*Sta buen*' [that is good] ! But move back. I 'm sitting horrid."

" Won 't I fall off ? "

" Won 't you — pooh ! Are all girls afraid in Old Knollsboro ? "

" I — don't — know."

" I hope not. I 've had a great cur'osity to see another girl besides myself, but I never did, — that is, to talk to 'em. If they 're all so scarey as you, I shall be awful dis'pointed."

" You 're a nasty, mean, hateful thing ! So there ! "

" Why — what ? " The face which Steenie turned toward her companion showed not the

slightest resentment, but the sincerest astonishment. "What did I do?"

"You said I was 'scarey' — and — and —
things!"

"But are n't you? I thought so. May be I
was mistookened. But Kinks thinks it's time
to go. Are you ready? What's your name?"

"Beatrice. Ye — es. I — guess — so. Won't
he — run away — again?"

"He'll run like a coyote! But he won't
behave bad any more. Ready?"

"Ye — es."

"Now, then! *Pronto* [get on]!" Away dashed
Kinks, bearing his double burden, as if determined to make up lost time, or to show the racing quality of his blood; but, swift as was his
pace, he was no longer wild, and seemed but another young thing, such as those who rode him,
overflowing with spirit and vitality.

"Ah, how good it seems! A'most like Tito!"

"Ye — es. I — I like it!" assented Beatrice,
so exhilarated by the rapid motion that she forgot
her fear.

"Which way now?" — as they came to the
turn of the road.

"Down there, through the iron gate."

"Is it his home, — and yours?"

" Yes."

" Then I 'll give him his head ; " and dropping
the bridle-rein upon his shoulders, Steenie folded
her arms while Kinks trotted more and more
slowly over the gravel road, till he stopped, of
his own accord, before the block where he was
accustomed to be mounted.

Both children were speedily off upon the
ground, and Steenie, feeling more at home and
happier than at any time since she had parted
from her four-footed friends at Santa Felisa,
began examining the various straps and buckles
of the gray's harness, with a professional air
which greatly impressed the watchful Beatrice.

" Who saddled this poor fellow ? "

" I — I don't know."

" You ought to know, then !   See here !
There 's a thorn in this surcingle.   That 's all
how it happened ! "

" That — little thing ?   And that big horse ? "

The groom has ridden up by this time, and
Steenie turned upon him swiftly.   " See here,
man !   I found this in the band ! "

" Well.   What of it ? "

" That 's what made him act up."

" That is too small to have been felt."

" I think not.   See ? "   The child struck the

brier sharply into the flesh of her own brown
little hand, and a red flush followed the wound.
"That has hurt him ever since he went out. Bob
says nothing's so sensitive as a horse; and then
something frightened him; and then he — ran
away. So would I, — if anything kept doing
this all the time!" And again she attacked her
own skin, — now so energetically that the blood
oozed out; at which she turned and clasped the
soft nostrils of the thorough-bred before her with
a tender pitying touch, and laid her own bonny
face caressingly against the face of the beast,
who stood in motionless enjoyment of this new
sympathy.

Nobody knew that a fourth person had observed this scene till a grave voice quietly asked :
"Little girl, who are you?"

Then the curly head was reluctantly lifted
from its resting-place, and a pair of radiant eyes
were raised toward the porch where the questioner stood. "I'm only Steenie Calthorp."

"Only — the most wonderful child I ever
saw! Where did you come from?"

"Santa Felisa, California."

"What are you doing here?"

Memory returned to her. What, indeed, was
she doing there, when she had been told by

her grandmother that she must be ready in just half-an-hour to "go and buy some decent clothes"!

"*Caramba!* I forgot!" And away flashed a white frock and a streaming mass of curly hair, without so much as a good-by to any of these new acquaintances.

CHAPTER VII.

STEENIE had little difficulty in retracing her way along the avenue as far as that old street of the town on which her grandmother's house stood; but there she stopped, confused.

"It was a big white house with a lion on

STEENIE AND HER GRANDMOTHER.

it." Alas! they were all big white houses in that locality, and more than one had a "lion on it."

"There is a white fence before it, and green blinds."

So were there everywhere, — for this staid, aristocratic, inland borough was nothing if not correct.   Years and years before, when it was young, its then leader of society had builded him a "mansion," standing so many paces back from the street, of such a width and stature. He had placed about the yard a protecting paling, white, — to match the house; with its green blinds which did not match the grass, but stared at it in a hardness of tone, so utterly green, that it made nature's color look yellow, — maybe from envy.

The example set in that far-away time continued still.   To the one big square white house succeeded other big, square, white houses, as like to the pattern as rule and measure could make them; to the ugly green blinds other rows of ugly green blinds; while the original paling stretched out far, far on either side.

Thus the great High Street of Old Knollsboro began and grew; and now was far too loyal to its past to alter its own cleanly and roomy monotony for any modern freaks of architecture.

It was on this thoroughfare that a strange little girl, who had never been lost on the wide plains of Santa Felisa, now stood looking about in awe-stricken perplexity.   She began, also, to feel physically very miserable.   Clouds had obscured the sun, and the wind had risen chilly, blowing through her light attire with a piercing breath new to her experience, and most unpleasant. Her shoes were water-soaked, and her feet stiff with the cold; and such a terrible forlornness suddenly overcame her that she felt very much like crying.

"But if I cry I can't see anything, then!" said this practical small creature, and forthwith restrained her tears. "Well, it must be further'n this, anyhow; an' if I go on, maybe I'll see a Maltese cat. Mary Jane says her cat is pure Malty; and so — Ho! There she goes!"

Thinking wholly of the animal which was to be her guide, Steenie pursued a fleeing object that she believed to be Mary Jane's possession; but she was disappointed at the very gateway of successful capture, beneath which the cat darted and through which the child would have followed but for the latch; about this her observant eye detected a radical difference from that of Madam Calthorp's.

"Hm-m, Miss Cat! You've run away again, I s'pose. Mary Jane says you are always running away an' 'pestering the life out of her.' An', maybe, you're like me, — don't know where you do b'long. Never mind. I guess you'll find your way home again; so I'll go on."

Steenie was so oddly and thinly clothed for that season and climate that some curious eyes looked after her sturdy little figure, as she passed swiftly up the street, darting questioning glances at every residence; but nobody thought of offering guidance. For wasn't Old Knollsboro in morning attire? Besides, open curiosity concerning one's neighbors was a common thing, and belonged to the vulgar crowd which did not inhabit High Street. So she made the full length of one side the roadway and had crossed to return upon the other, when she spied in the distance a bent, blue-coated old man, whom she recognized at once.

"It's Mr. Tubbs! It truly is! Hurrah!" she cried, with a delight quite contrasting to the terror this same person had caused her earlier in the day. Then she sped forward till she had overtaken and thrown herself upon her victim's shoulders, who rebounded from the shock of the attack with a groan horrible to hear, but which no longer daunted the glad child. "Oh, you dear Mr. Resolved! Here you were, looking for me, and all the time I was—"

"Wasn't lookin' fer ye 't all! Oh, oh! Be ye born ter murder me outright, er be ye not? Um-m! That's what I'd like ter know."

"Murder you? Why, you · must be funny! How, why should a little girl murder anybody?"

"My-soul-I-declare! But you seem boun' ter! An' in the name o' common sense, what be ye doin' out here with no clothes on ter speak of? Where's yer bunnit er yer shawl?"

Shawl! Steenie had never thought of it from the moment when she took it off and laid it on the fence. The fence! What fence? Where? All up and down those two long rows of palings which faded into an indistinct line and seemed to melt together in the distance, the child's eyes searched critically. But there was nothing in sight to suggest the shawl, which had been only loaned by Madam Calthorp, and Steenie's fear took a new direction. What if it were lost? — as she had been, and the Maltese cat.

She had been trained to a very nice observance of "thine" and "mine;" and even at Santa Felisa, where she was so universally loved and indulged, she had never mislaid or used anything belonging to another without permission. How dreadful to begin now with something owned by that stern, beautiful grandmother whom she already loved so dearly, yet who seemed too "intelligy" to return such a simple sentiment!

"Which is my grandmother's house, Mr. Resolved? Please, will you show me? — even if you were n't sent after me."

"Sent arter ye! Humph! Psst-t! I 'd like ter see myself bein' sent arter younguns, at my time o' life!"

"Where, please? Quick!"

For answer the old man pushed his spectacles into their legitimate place and looked at the questioner searchingly. "Well, I hate ter own it, but I s'pose I 'll have ter. I 'lowed ter Mary Jane fust off, 't ye did n't seem like common younguns; an' then that fool kind o' talk this mornin'; an' now, a losin' of yerself in a plain straight road like this. It 's a pity, — it 's a terr'ble pity."

"Of course it is. But don't you see? I did it just because it *is* so plain. I was never outside my grandmother's house before, only when we came. And I was so tired I did n't notice; an' these rows and rows look just like a flock of sheep, each more the same than the other; and if you won't tell me" — A fit of shivering cut short her remarks.

"Gracious! You ain't a ketchin' cold, be ye? A'ready? This way, then, suddent! Er there ye 'll be ter be nussed." With which humble imitation of his mistress' sentiments, Mr. Tubbs faced about, and seizing Steenie's cold little hand, hurried back to their own domicile as fast as age and lumbago would permit.

"Now, look a here. Take a notice. Ye may n't be bright, but ye can l'arn sunthin', an' I 'm boun' ter teach ye.   That gate-latch has a round quirl on the top.   See? an' there hain't another gate-latch has a nothin' but a square quirl the hull endurin' length o' High Street.   Do ye understan' what I 'm a sayin'?"

"Why, yes, certainly.   Why should n't I?" laughed Steenie, forgetting her fear of her guide in gratitude for his "kindness" in returning her to her friends, and wondering why he thought her so slow of comprehension.   But no sooner was the "round quirled" latch lifted than she darted past him and in at the front door, which, for an unusual thing, stood wide open.

"Papa! Grandmother! Where are you? I 'm so glad — I 'm sorry — I lost it — I was lost, too, and he 's — the loveliest great gray — Papa! Papa Calthorp!"

Her father emerged from the library, looking very pale and careworn; but she sprang into his arms with such exuberant delight that a smile rose to his lips.   Then he clasped her close, — closer than she had ever known him to do, and his cheek felt the chill of hers.   "Why, sweetheart, how cold you are! Where have you been?"

"Did n't you hear, Papa, dear? I said I had been lost."

Very speedily thereafter Steenie found herself in bed. She did n't quite comprehend it, and it certainly was her first experience of going into such retirement in the daytime; but one glance at the child's wet feet and shivering body had alarmed Madam greatly.

"Right out of that warm climate into this, and clad as she is! This way, Steenie, at once. Oh, your shoes! The tracks on the carpet!"

"Here, darling, I'll carry you;" and as directly as if his eyes could see, Mr. Calthorp bore his little girl to her own room and himself assisted in tucking her into the thick blankets, while Mary Jane fussed about with hot bricks and soap-stones, and Madam Calthorp administered a dose of sage-tea, whose aroma carried the father back to the days of his own childhood.

When the excitement had somewhat subsided, and Steenie had assured them over and over that she was as "warm as a pepper-stew," the house-mistress sat down to listen to the tale which her grandchild had, until then, vainly endeavored to tell.

" First, I 'm so sorry about your shawl. I took
it off, 'cause it was so warm ; an' I don't know
where the place was. The fence is just the same,
and — "

" Never mind the shawl, Steenie ; it is certain
to be returned. Somebody will find and recog-
nize it; but what is that about a horse ? "

Holding fast to her father's hand, Steenie gave
a graphic description of the runaway, and its result. When she had finished, Madam sat in
a silence which was plainly that of a shocked
dismay. Finally she spoke.

" This is even worse than I feared. No such
accident must occur again. Steenie, before another word is said, promise me that you will not
go into the street again without permission."

" No, no, Mother ! " interposed Mr. Calthorp,
earnestly. "Pardon my disputing your authority, but that will not answer. Steenie has never
known restraint, and — but let us settle all this
at some other time."

The lady sighed. She had her own ideas of how
a little girl should be brought up; but she felt
her old hands inadequate to the task. She had
been so peaceful and free ! Why had this trial
been sent upon her ? Gravely she arose and left
the room, and the relieved runaway went to sleep,

to wake at the dinner hour with no worse feeling about her than rebellion against being kept in bed when there was " nothing the matter that ever was."

The immediate result of that morning's adventure, so far as Steenie was concerned, was a suitable wardrobe. A dressmaker took up her abode in the west chamber, and there the restless child was imprisoned during a fortnight of bright days, while birds sang invitations to her through the windows, and the crocuses coaxed her with their shining faces to "come out of doors and be glad!"

But the only time she could command for that was after the crocuses and the birds had gone to sleep, and the dressmaker had stopped work for the day.

"Why do I need so many things, dear grandmother? I'm sure they're pretty; but — "

"Many, Steenie? I have never been an extravagant woman, and I certainly shall not cultivate the habit now. But there must be two comfortable school-frocks and three or four thinner ones; for I wish everything to be accomplished at once that will be required during the summer. There must be a simple dress for church and a richer one for visiting; and — that is all.

I 'm sure you are the first little girl I ever knew
who did n't like handsome clothes."

" Oh, you have n't known even me — that
way! For I like the frocks well enough, but not
the fixing of them. I stand up, ' being fitted,'
till my feet ache like anything ; and Miss Ses-
sions' knuckles have punched me all over black
and blue. She does n't mean it, of course ; but
when she puts in a pin she jams against me like
I was her lap-board. And I wish needles had n't
eyes ! 'Cause I 'most put mine out threading 'em."

" Why, Steenie ! I thought you were a contented child ! I have never heard you complain
of anything before."

" Have n't you ? Am I complaining ? But
— it 's — it 's — awfully, awfully lonesome ! I
wish Papa would come back ! I can't sleep
nights for wondering about his poor eyes ; and
how long it will take the man to fix 'em. "

" There, there ! That-will do. Don't allow
yourself to give way to habits of despondency.
Your father expected to be gone for two weeks,
and he has been for but for ten days. Maybe, if you
go down into the kitchen, you can see Mary Jane
get supper."

" Yes 'm," said Steenie, choking back her emotion, and turning toward the stairs, whence,

seeing her grandmother stoop to pick up a thread from the carpet, she ran to save her the trouble, and ended by throwing her arms about the silk-clad shoulders and giving them a hearty squeeze. "Oh! I do love you so, Grandmother!"

"Why, Steenie? Because of the new frocks and pretty jackets?"

"Grandmother! How funny! 'Cause of nothing at all only — 'cause!"

At which senseless reason the giver of it smiled merrily, and the recipient smiled almost indulgently.

"Well, run now! To-morrow you will be at school, and a new life will begin for you."

"How? Am I not living now?"

"In one way, yes. But there is a world of books to which your school training will open the door. To me, that world is everything, or was. I find — some other things — begin to interest me now."

"What things, Grandmother?"

"No matter, little questioner; but things utterly different from any printed page." When Madam Calthorp said anything that Steenie did not understand, the latter readily attributed it to the lady's great "intelligence," which she had now learned to call by its right name.

But, somehow, that little talk had set both old and young hearts to lighter beating; and Steenie departed kitchen-ward, feeling that "watching Mary Jane" was something interesting, even if it could not quite equal a race on the sands with Tito.

But of that beloved animal she dared not think often. It was apt to make a troublesome "ache" come "in her throat," and it "did n't do any good."

On the following morning, feeling very curious and happy, Steenie entered the primary department of the great school for which Old Knollsboro was famous. She did not know that girls "going on eleven" usually disdained "primaries" as far beneath them, and she would n't have cared if she had; but, at the first recess, she was enlightened on the subject by a young miss in braids, who remarked, patronizingly, "Oh, you 're the new girl, are n't you?"

"I 'm not new, — not very. I 'm over ten."

"What? I don't mean new that way. You just came."

"No. I have been here ever so long. Grandmother says 'bout three weeks."

"Don't you feel mad to go with the little ones?"

" No.   I think I like little ones best.   I never saw any 'bout my size 'cept Beatrice, and — and — you," concluded Steenie, stammering in her confusion over saying something that even to her untrained ears sounded " not just right."

" My!   Aren't you polite!   Well, what can you expect, my mother says, of a girl that's lived in California amongst cow-boys."

" Cow-boys are nicer — nicer than — nice!   I love them, every one ! " cried this loyal Santa Felisan.

" You'd ought to be ashamed ! "

" Why ? "

" Oh, because.   Say, has Beatrice Courtenay been to see you ? "

" Yes.   Once."

" You thought you did something smart, did n't you?   Ma said it was disgraceful for a girl to get talked about like you have been."

Steenie stared in amazement, then bethought herself of her grandmother's parting advice : " Be pleasant to all, as is natural to you ; but do not have much to say to any girl until you have learned her name.   I wish you to make only the right friends, and I can tell you about all the families — if not all the children — in town.   It is wise to select your playmates from households of gentlewomen. 'Even a child is known by the company he keeps.'"

"Will you please tell me your name, miss girl?"

"It's Annie Gibson. My father keeps a candy store."

"Does he? Why does that bell ring? Is n't the lady pretty who teaches me? She thinks I read very well indeed, for — for — me."

"Pooh! You'd ought to hear me! I'm in the Fifth Reader. I speak pieces, examination days. Your dress is awful nice and stylish. I bet you did n't have that made in your old California. I bet your grandmother had to give it to you."

"Annie, you should n't say 'I bet.' Grandmother c'rected me, myself, for doing it. My grandmother is a very in-tell-i-gent woman, my father says, an' I'm to watch out for the way she talks; 'cause she never says anything 'nelegant. But I think your frock is pretty, too. It's redder 'n mine, an' more ruffley, is n't it? I think you are very nice to look at. Your eyes are black, are n't they? And your hair is nice an' straight. An' what beautiful big feet you have, an' hands! Why, your hands are a'most twice as big 's mine!'"

Poor Annie Gibson did n't know whether to laugh or " get mad ; " but there was no doubting the sincere and admiring curiosity with which Steenie Calthorp examined this other specimen of girlhood ; but the final tones of the bell called both away toward the house.

Which, however, Steenie did not enter. Her attention had suddenly been attracted by a commotion in the street, and everything new appealed to her curiosity.

" My ! I wonder what those boys are doing ! What — What — What ! "

With a shriek of delight that penetrated the building she was deserting, the child darted from the enclosure, — through the crowd of grinning boys straight to the cause of all their mirth. " My Sutro ! My Sutro ! My own, ownest Tito ! "

" *Caramba !* My angel ! Is it thou ? At last — at last ! "

CHAPTER VIII.

STEENIE AND TITO.

SUTRO and Tito, indeed! The former in the full glory of his holiday Mexican costume, looking a little the worse for a long journey; the latter in exuberant spirits over his release from the car which he had occupied for nearly a week, padded and luxurious though it had been. The extravagant caresses of one old friend, and the pleading, loving neighings of the other, were met by an ecstatic response, which told how greatly they had been missed.

"Oh! How — Why — I'm so glad I shall — cry!"

"Santa Maria! We part no more, *mi niña* [my little one]."

" But how could you come ? You darlings ! "

" How ? Save on that horrible railway train,
de veras, indeed ! But thy Tito suffered not at
all, he. Bob and the boys sent him to thee, their
Little Un ; for, in verity, he was of no use to the
Lord of Plunkett, no. Not a saddle nor a bridle
would he endure, until to-day. And so — goes
thy Bob to the señor and says : ' The Little Un's
horse travels east to the Little Un, with old
Sutro, who will not live at San' Felisa without
his heart's dearest.' And — here we are. *Caramba!* Thou lookest fine, no ? But — still —
thou wilt return with Sutro to the old *hacienda,*
wilt thou not, *mañana* [to-morrow, sometime] ? "

" The very first *mañana* that ever I can !
But, go away, you boys ! What do you want
with us ? "

" A circus ! A circus ! " cried the gamins,
delighted at seeing Steenie now mounted behind
the old Spaniard, whose striking apparel re-
minded them of nothing but the fascinating
entertainment just mentioned.

" It 's that horse girl ! "

" It 's her that rode Beatrice Courtenay's
runaway ! "

" I 'll bet all my alleys she does b'long to a
circus, an' that 's another of 'em ! "

"Say, Sissy, what show you skedaddle out of? Give us the tip!"

"The tip, no? The whole of it, you miserables!" Suiting the action to the word, Sutro leaned sidewise from the saddle, and laid about him hastily with his short riding-whip. This had the effect of ridding them from immediate persecution, and, taking advantage of this lull in the attentions of the street boys, Steenie gave Tito his word of command, and away they shot at a pace to distance all pursuers.

Madam Calthorp looked up from her book as the clattering of horse-hoofs fell on the gravel of the path which led to her disused stable, and could scarcely believe her own eyes for the story they told her.

She was still trembling from the shock of her surprise when Steenie bounded into her presence, wild with excitement and radiantly glad. "O, Grandmother — Grandmother! Who do you think has come? Tito — Tito — Tito! My own Tito! And that blessed old Sutro, who is as old as old, but did n't mind anything but staying away from his *niña!* Come — come — quick — and see them!"

She could not stand still, not one instant; but around and around her grandmother's chair she danced, while that lady slowly rose, wondering at herself for even this concession.

" This way ! This way ! To the — I s'pose it 's the stable ! And won't Tito be glad to get into a quiet stall once more ?   And the grass !   Can he roll on the cunning little lawn, Grandmother ? "

" Steenie, silence.   Be still for one moment. What is all this ?   Who is ' Tito,' who ' Sutro ' ? Why are you not at school ? "

" Why — why — I don't know.   I s'pose I for-got.   Sutro — is Sutro.   Don't you know I told you 'bout him ?   He 's my body-servant, and as old as anything.   But such a rider !   There 's nobody in all San' Felisa can beat him, 'cept Kentucky Bob an' some more.   Bless his heart ! Bob's, I mean.   Bless everybody's !   For he 's come all these long three thousand miles to bring me my pretty piebald Tito.   The Plunketty Lord said he should always be mine, case I ever went back ; but those dear boys would n't wait for that — no !   I s'pose they saw that Tito was breaking his heart and s'posed I was mine ; and so they paid all the money for Tito's ticket, and hired him a beautiful cushioned horse-box, and sent Sutro to take care of him till he brought him safe to me.   And — and — he 's — they 're never going away any more till I go,

too.   Oh, *hola, hola!*   Are n't you glad — glad
— glad ? "

If she were glad she did not so express herself ;
nor did Madam Calthorp's countenance exhibit
any emotion brighter than dismayed astonishment as she followed this strange child out of
the room and out of the house, in order to be
presented to two more intruders.

" Sutro, Caballero Don Sutro Vives, this is my
beautiful Madam Grandmother.   And Tito — my
sweet ! "

" I have the honor to kiss thy feet, Señora,"
said the old Spaniard, bowing profoundly.

For a moment Madam regarded him with admiring curiosity.   As a " type " of that race which
she had read of in history, a race that was fast
dying out, he interested her, and for that reason
she was glad to see him ; and the caballero,
lifting his eyes from the ground, beheld only the
pleasure, and did not question its cause.   " The
Doña Steenie says truly, Madam ; the Señora is
beautiful, — as the snows on the Sierras.   May
the humblest of her slaves beg her gracious
favor ? "

Such language was new to Old Knollsboro,
though to Steenie's ears it was as familiar and as
meaningless as the ordinary salutations of the

day to other folk; and she interrupted any reply
which Madam might have made by seizing that
lady's hand and placing it on Tito's flowing mane.
"Isn't it fine and white, — whiter and softer
than the freshest fleece ever sheared ? And see
the pretty, pretty markings all over his body!
Lift your foot, my Tito. One — two — three —
four ! One — two — three — four ! Isn't that
a fine action ? And his haunches ! See how
strong and shapely. And his lovely tail, set
straight and free ! And his darling neck ! Oh,
my Tito, I love you! I love you!"

Madam Calthorp was speechless. Not only
was she amazed, but she was touched. She had
never seen anything like this. It was as if a
twin had found its mate; and the exchange of
sentiment between the two young creatures was
too evident for even her untrained eyes to ignore.
Steenie was not one whit more glad than Tito;
nor did she express her emotion more clearly.
The animal's velvet nostrils moved everywhere
about the curly head and bobbing shoulders of
his recovered mistress, with an exquisite gentle-
ness of touch she could not have believed possible
in "only a horse." There was adoring delight
in the great brown eyes which followed Steenie's
every motion, and seemed blind to all else; and

when Sutro had unfastened the stable door, the loving pair went joyfully away together, her arm about his neck, bent proudly to receive it.

" My-soul-I-declare ! "

This ejaculation, in the harshest utterance of Mr. Resolved Tubbs, broke in upon this pretty scene with the force of an explosion. It cleared the air of undue sentiment, and recalled Madam Calthorp to a sense of her position and its consequences. Here she had not only received these unwelcome intruders, but allowed them to believe that she was glad to do so! She must right the mistake at once.

" Ahem, Mr. Sutro, I mean Vives, I think it would be better to take that animal directly to the livery stable. I do not keep a horse, and should not be willing to let Steenie. As for yourself, while your devotion is touching, I think you can find more comfortable quarters at the village than I can give you. This man — Tubbs, will you show this old gentleman the way to the American House ? "

Considering the lumbago, Mr. Tubbs stepped forward with amazing alacrity. He was quite willing to prevent his small " world " being " turned upside down " by this fresh consignment from the far west. But his obliging readiness fell powerless before the caballero's obtuse serenity.

"Ten thousand pardons, most charming Señora, but whatever will serve my hostess serves me. Old Sutro is not particular."

"But — gracious!" retorted Resolved, and began an explanation which was cut short by Steenie's reappearance with the request : "Please get me some alfalfa, or oats, or something for my Tito's dinner; will you, Mr. Tubbs?"

"Steenie, there is nothing for a horse to eat here. I have not kept one in many years. The last one was your father's, before he left home. This animal must be taken elsewhere for the present."

"Grandmother! My Tito? After so long, long a journey? Oh, no, no, no!"

"But, my child, be reasonable. The stable is —"

"'Xcuse my interrupting, but it's just as nice as nice. They's a lovely box-stall, only wants taking those old rubbishy things out of it; an' places for everything. We can go to the shop where you buy things for horses, and buy him all he needs. Same's you bought my clothes. An' then such fun! Won't Papa be glad! And Sutro — forgive me not thinking 'bout you, too.

Are you hungry, dear Sutro? You're 'most always, don't you know?"

"Ah, Señorita! The food on the way was not of Ellen's sort. In verity, I would like a dish of —"

"A'most anything, no? Grandmother, may Mary Jane cook Sutro some dinner?"

"Hm. It must be near the dinner-hour for all of us; and you may invite your old friend for this one meal." The significance of the lady's tone was not lost upon her ancient servitor, Resolved, but it was — wholly — upon the happy unconsciousness of these two reunited comrades, whom Madam Calthorp watched with growing interest; even herself forgetting, as Steenie had utterly forgotten, that there was such a thing as school and its duties.

"She is a different creature! Vivacious, sparkling, charming. And all for that queer old man and queerer horse! Is it as my son has thought and said, — that the key to the child's nature is love, — overflowing love? Well, there is, certainly, no mistaking the love between those two nor the want of it between these — two!" considered the unwilling hostess, turning her eyes upon the two old men, as Sutro and Resolved glared with instant and mutual dislike upon each other.

" Can it be possible that Tubbs is actually growing fond of the child, and is jealous ? "

It seemed so, strange as it was ; for when
dinner was served, and Sutro, naturally, took his
place behind Steenie's chair, the other ancient
worthy remarked with considerable sharpness :
" Ye kin set down, can't ye ? " and pointedly
pushed a chair back to designate where.

" Ten thousand thanks, my friend ; when the
Señorita has finished," answered Sutro, suavely.

" Sin-your-eet-her, hey ? What heathen gibber-
ish is that, I 'd like ter know ? Thar 's yer place,
an' thar ye kin set er go 'ithout, — uther one,"
retorted Tubbs, forgetting in his aversion to this
" furriner " the respect due to the occasion.

" *Luego* [presently]." With the sweetest of
smiles, old Vives, who had been watching Resolved's manner of service, deftly turned his
little lady's plate, exactly as the other had done
Madam Calthorp's.

When Mr. Tubbs passed to his mistress the
food which Mary Jane had carved, the stranger
anticipated a similar attention to Steenie. So
with everything ; till even the house-mistress's
dignity yielded to a smile, and the little girl
laughed outright.

" Why, you two funny men ! What makes

you go snap — snap — with things, so? And poor Mr. Resolved, if it's your lumbago worse, just let Sutro take care of Grandmother, too. My Sutro can do everything beau-u-tifully; can't you, dear?"

"*Si?* It is music thou speakest, *carita.*"

"T-wu-ho!" With this indescribable snort Mr. Tubbs retreated to the kitchen and threw himself down recklessly in Mary Ann's own rocker. But the rocker was cushioned, and Resolved was tired; and the combination revealed the fact that even an enemy has his uses. "My-soul-I-declare! If he wants ter trot round waitin' on younguns, let him trot! Ain't no law ag'in it, as I know of."

"Ner ag'in your behavin' like a great, cross youngun yerself, if I do say so!" said Mary Jane, dishing apple-fritters with a skilful hand.

"Ain't cross. An' if I be, ain't it enough ter make a critter a'most sw'ar? Here was we livin' like pigs in clover; and in come Mr. Daniel an' the gal. Now, 's if that wa'n't upsettin' enough — piles in a heathen Mexican an' a calico horse ter boot! I do say, an' I mean it, folks does sometimes get more o' trouble 'n they desarve in this world."

"Calico horses is lucky. Hain't you never

heerd that? I always wish when I see one, an'
that ain't often. An', though it does make a
pile o' work, I — no, sir! — I ain't a mite sorry 't
Mr. Dan'l an' Steenie come!"

"Ma-ry-Ja-ne!" Tubbs half rose from his
chair, in astonishment at his sister's words.
"An' you — a perfessor!"

"Perfessor from my youth up," assented the
spinster, piously. "That's why it's borne in on
me ter witness fer the truth. I hated it — Here!
you Mr. Sutry! Jest fetch all them things out,
fust. Don't leave anything on the table, savin' the
bread an' the salt. And — there ye be! Handy
as a womern, I do declare! — Yes, sir, I hated it
wuss 'n pisen. So 't I couldn't sleep, worryin'
'bout the victuals ter cook an' the dishes ter wash,
an' the hull job. An' I knowed Madam hated it
even wusser. But now — mebbe it's grace 'at's
'gin me, an' mebbe it's only natur'; but that
little creetur has 'bout changed the hull outlook
o' things. She jest acted as if I loved her the
terr'blest 't ever was, an' fust I knowed — I did!
Thar wasn't no holdin' out ag'in them big inner-
cent eyes o' her 'n, a smilin' so right inter a body
till a body can't help smilin' back. So — now
I 've told it out, an' I feel better. You b'lieve
my words, brother Resolved, an' mark 'em well:

Thar's a blessin' come with poor Mr. Dan'l's comin', an' it's took visible shape in that thar child!"

" Well — I swan!"

" Hm-m. Ye need n't 'swan' nothin'. Madam's through. Come along an' eat yer dinner. An' remember ter let yer candle burn afore that poor, yaller-skinned, heathen stranger, who, if he hain't got the grace o' perfessorship has got it o' perliteness."

Thus adjured, "professor" Tubbs arose and followed Mary Jane into the dining-room, where Sutro had already seated himself in the chair designated by his new *confrère,* and was smiling blandly kitchen-wards, when that person's bent figure darkened the doorway. But if there was any spiritual light-shining or candle-burning, it was not of a sort to impress the Catholic Christian with the beauty of the Puritan creed.

Alas! It was war from the beginning with these two; and, though both were inwardly conscious of their own blame in the matter, no amount of self-abusive prayers on one side or muttered Ave Marias on the other could ever change the course of nature.

" Water won't run up-hill; an' folks 'at 's

born contrary stays contrary. All you kin expect is ter keep the peace," said the shrewd
Mary Jane, and determined to make a bridge of
her own patience which should serve both sides
of the hostile camp.

After dinner the question of Tito again arose;
and, pending her son's return, Madam compro-
mised her own judgment and sent off an order
for food and bedding sufficient for a few days'
need. "I'm growing very weak and indulgent,"
she said, apologetically, to Mary Jane. "But
this arrival was so unexpected, it may be as well
to await Daniel's decision."

"Yes 'm. An' I do 'low you won't be sorry.
She don't ask ner tease fer nothin'; hain't never
sence she come. 'Bout them books, even; I've
seen her a marchin' back an' forth, back an'
forth, a lookin' through the glass at 'em that
longin' 'at I've be'n a'most a mind ter open the
bookcases an' show 'em to her. But, o' course, I
did n't; an' she did n't say ary word, ner even
look mad, only kinder hungry-like. 'T would be
a pity not ter let her have her pony, seems ter
me. Mr. Sutry, he says she kin beat any circuser
't ever was. She's rid' ever sence she was a
baby; an' them men out ter Californy — 'boys,'
she calls 'em — 'd a never let her come east in

the world if it had n't a be'n fer her pa's eyes.
When 's he comin' home, Ma'am?"

" Soon, I hope. And that he will be reassured
concerning his dreaded blindness. It cannot be
that a Calthorp — such a strong, healthy, handsome man he is, Mary Jane — should suffer such
a physical blemish!"

In that sentence spoke one of Madam Calthorp's strongest prejudices. Against imperfec-
tion of any sort her proud heart rebelled. Her
own physique was faultless. She wore her years
and her white hairs as royally as a queen her
ermine mantle. She had always prayed that she
might die thus, in her full vigor, before any
mortal weakness touched her; and her feeling of
this sort extended to all belonging to her. If
her son died, she would mourn him; but if he
lived, a helpless wreck, she dared not contemplate the prospect.

" No, it don't 'pear so; but the ' don't 'pear
so-s' are gen'ally what happens; an' though I
hate ter say it, I think you 'd oughter know that
Mr. Dan'l went away a'most convicted in his
own mind 'at he would n't never see no more o'
this mortal speer 'an he saw then."

" Mary Jane! But you are not always a true
prophet."

" An' I hope, with all that's in me, 'at I ain't now ! "

But — she was. An attendant brought Daniel Calthorp home that night; and the first glance which his mother cast upon his face disclosed that his last hope of restored sight had gone out from it.

CHAPTER IX.

THERE was no evading the fact that a terrible misfortune had fallen upon the Calthorp household; and, for a time, this great sorrow excluded every other thought. But they were all bravehearted, having that one quality in common; and so, even while suffering most acutely, Madam found that the feeling she had experienced in regard to her son's blindness faded in the light of the great pity which now filled her soul. She had feared that she could never bear to look upon him and witness his helplessness; but, instead of this being the case, she found herself watching him in silent admiration for the fortitude he displayed, and growing even prouder than before.

TITO.

"Well. Blind or seeing, he is still — a man! Able to support his own courage, and that of those who lean upon him! And how beautiful is Steenie's tenderness! She seems to understand that he wishes to do everything for himself which he can do; but her own bright eyes watch constantly to aid him in those he cannot."

Mary Jane, observing her mistress's face, and following the direction of her eyes, smiled, well pleased. Then she stole away to remark to Resolved: "You said we might 'bout as well gin up, when Mr. Dan'l come home that night an' laid his goggles off, 'cause they was n't no more use a pertectin' stun blindness no longer; but — they's some kinds o' onseeingness wuss'n ever ailded mortal eyes. An' that's sperritooal. Thar was Madam, a nussin' up wrath ag'in the day o' jedgment, jest 'cause her only had married somebody 't she had n't picked out fer him; an' him a cl'arin' out ter Californy with his wife, an' a buryin' her thar; an' a comin' back home this way he is. But I tell ye, brother Resolved, it was the plain doin's of the Lord, er my name ain't Tubbs!"

"Well, mebbe. I mean — o' course. I ain't a goin' back on my perfession; but some folks has got a terr'ble gift o' makin' sunthin' out o' nothin'. Did n't uset ter be yer way ter call bad

good; but, my-soul-I-declare! Ain't no makin'
ye out, now-a-days, ye 've growed that weak-
minded an' soft-spoke.   Howsomever, one thing
ye can't turn ner twist inter no great hilarity:
an' that 's that pesky Mexicer."

"I should like ter know why not? Ain't he jest
like a shadder ter Mr. Dan'l? If that poor deluded
popist critter ain't 'arnin' his board an' keep, I
know some other folks 'at ain't wuth their salt."

"Hm-m.   From the soond o' that, I conclude 'at
thar 's *some* — o' the 'riginal Mary Jane left, arter
all!" retorted the other, and doddered away.

It had seemed providential, indeed, that Sutro
Vives — old fellow though he was — had come
to them when he did.   With the profound love
which he had always felt for little Steenie, he
now turned to Steenie's father; and his wonderful vitality enabled him to discharge with perfect
ease tasks which would have fallen very heavily
upon poor Resolved Tubbs.

Another two weeks had passed; and they had
all, in a measure, become accustomed to Mr. Calthorp's affliction, and to the coming of the "four
Westerners," — as Mary Jane called the three human visitors and the equine one, — when Steenie
came home from school a picture of childish
distress.

"I can't — can't — can't — go to that horrid school! Never no more, never!" with which exclamation she burrowed into the nest her father's arms made for her, and hid her tearful face on his breast.

He waited until her sobs had subsided, and then inquired: "Why not, darling?"

"Because — oh, 'cause — I hate it! Maybe that's bad, but I do. The children go 'buz-z, buz-z' over their books; and it's hot; and I can't breathe, a'most; and, oh, Papa, I want to go home!"

"My little one, I shall have to forbid your 'boys' writing to you, if their letters make you homesick."

"It isn't that. It isn't, really, truly. But — am I a 'runaway circuser,' Papa, dear?"

"Why, no. Certainly not. Why should you need contradiction of such a silly charge?"

"'Cause that's what they all call me — 'most every one. An' they say: 'Why won't you give us a ride on your old Spot-back, Californy!' And: 'She's the girl 'at's only in the Primary! 'Cause she's brought up in a stable;' an' such heaps o' mean things that I feel — I feel 's if I should suff'cate. Need I go, Papa, dearest?"

"I cannot tell yet. Let us talk it over with Grandmother. Rather, I will do that, and you do what is far more to your liking and better for you,— wash away your tears, find Sutro, and tell him he may go for a horse at the livery-stable; then jump on Tito's back and ride your troubles away."

When obedience is happiness, it is always prompt; but even happiness has its drawbacks. It was this very riding on the piebald horse which had excited the envy and malice of a few of Old Knollsboro small folks. The majority of Steenie's school-fellows were full of an unexpressed admiration for her wonderful horsemanship as exhibited in the — to her quiet — rides through the village streets; but she was not the first person who has forgotten the flavor of the grapes in the sting of the wasp hidden among them, — although, heretofore, her sunny nature had risen above her annoyances with its own gay rebound.

Now, when she had ridden out of the yard, and the merry tones of her farewell had satisfied her father's ear that all was well for the present, he went "to talk it over," as he had promised, with the mother, whom he now consulted in all things.

"Well, Daniel, this is very strange! It seems like a Providence. I have observed Steenie closely; and I am sorry to say that the school plan has not worked as successfully as I had hoped. She does n't know what is the matter; but I do. It is the unwonted confinement. She asked Mary Jane what a prison was like; and when it was described, said: 'Oh, I thought, maybe, it was like our school-house.' It is really very opportune."

"But what, Mother? I do not understand."

"This morning's call from Mrs. Courtenay. She says the Judge was so pleased with Steenie, and that Beatrice talks so much about her, they beg me to allow our little girl to go to Rookwood every day and share their child's instruction and amusement. That two such lonely only children can do each other a deal of good. What do you say?"

"Yes, with all my heart. If you approve."

"It does seem an admirable arrangement. The Judge has always expressed his deep obligation to your father for assistance when his own prospects were poor; and I can understand a proud man's desire to render some recognition of this 'claim,' — though such, I am sure, I have never felt it. Steenie will have only the most helpful surround-

ings at Rookwood; and she will be fully appreciated.   I am glad, very glad."

"Why, Mother!   Your voice sounds as if you
— actually — loved my little one."

"I do, my son."

"And have you quite forgiven her likeness to
her mother?"

There was a moment's pause.   Then Daniel
Calthorp felt his mother's kiss upon his cheek,
and, in that rare caress, died from both hearts
all bitter memories.

Mary Jane witnessed this little incident through
a crack in the door.   Alas, Mary Jame was a
"mortal woman!"   Then she stole away with
misty eyes, — misty, perhaps, from the strain of
peeping, — murmuring piously: "And a little
child shall lead 'em."

But her piety did not prevent her being the
first to meet Steenie on her return from the ride,
and imparting the intelligence which was the result of Mrs. Courtenay's visit, instead of leaving
that pleasant business to those whose own it
really was.

"You ain't never a goin' back to no more
prisony-school, at all, Steenie Calthorp!"

"Why — not?   Will Papa let me stay home
every day?"

"No. But trot along an' hear. I ain't a goin' ter take the good news out o' nobody's mouth, I guess!"

For once, neglecting to care for her play-fellow, Tito, Steenie bounded in-doors, eager to have Mary Jane's statement confirmed; which being done, her pleasure knew no limits.

"Why, Papa Calthorp! It 'll be a'most the same as San' Felisa! They 's a great big house, forty times bigger 'n this, an' a great big grass all round it; an' trees, an' flower-beds, an' hammocks, an' — an' — things! And Sutro must go, too; an' I 'll ride Tito. An' sometimes, maybe, the Judge 'll let me go into the fields where the horses are. I 've seen them, dozens of them — beauties — corralled, I mean paddocked, in cute little places with green fences around them, an' a reg'lar shed for them to go under when it rains. Just like some o' the girls play 'house' at recess. Oh, do you s'pose he will?"

"I do not doubt it. Especially as he loves horses almost as well as you, and sympathy of tastes makes ready friendships. I foresee a very happy road to learning for you, my Steenie."

With this assurance in her ears, the child went gayly away on Tito's back toward Rookwood, with Sutro walking beside her at a pace which

Resolved Tubbs could never have equalled, even in his youth.

"Oh, Steenie, how glad I am!" cried Beatrice, for welcome. "Mama says we are to have our lessons out of doors; 'cause it's good for me, an' what you 're used to, as well."

"Only I never had lessons at all, till I came to Old Knollsboro! But just learned to read an' write a little. An' do you think your father will ever let me go to see his horses?"

"I b'lieve you care more for them than for anything! You funny girl!" answered Beatrice, reprovingly. "You 're just the same as he is; an' Mama says horses are to my father what play-hour is to school-boys. I don't know 'xactly what she means — but — he loves them, anyway."

"Course he does. He couldn't help it, could he?"

"Mama can help it. She says she 'xpects some of us 'll get killed; 'specially with Diablo, that 'xpensive colt. He is n't anything — yet; never had anything on him, even a halter; but Papa says, 'he must be broken, if he scours the country to find somebody brave enough to do it!'"

"Diablo? Oh, he 's the one 'at 'most killed the groom, is n't he?"

"Yes. An' he's kicked a whole lot of folks. He's out in his paddock all alone; and the men just give him food and water, an' let him stay there. Mama says that he ought to be shot, and then he could n't hurt anybody else."

"Why! How dreadful!"

"What? To hurt folks?"

"To shoot a beautiful fellow like Diablo. I've looked at him over the fence, when I've been riding with Sutro; and he is the finest horse in Old Knollsboro."

"How do you know that?"

"Well, he's the finest one I've seen here, yet. He has better points, even, than Gray Monarch, Kentucky Bob's thoroughbred."

"My! That's what Papa calls him : thoroughbred; an' says when he's trained he'll be su-perb. But I'd like to know who'll do it. Say. Is that old man coming to school too? Who is he? Is n't he queer? He's as wizzly-up as can be; but he makes me think of grasshoppers, he's so awful jumpy an' quick."

Steenie laughed. "He's my body-servant, he says; but he's a real 'ristocratic. He's a Californian, like they used to be, and a caballero. But after my mother died, he gave up everything but taking care of me. He's a perfect darling."

"Is he?" asked Beatrice, doubtfully. "He does n't look very — very pretty; but, I mean he 's beautiful, of course, only — here 's Ma'am-selle! Now for b-a-ba k-e-r-ker, baker; p-a-pa pay-e-r, I mean p-e-r-per. Do you like to spell?"

"No. It makes me awful dizzy."

"Me, too. But 'rithmetic 's more worser. Never mind. The quicker we get done, the quicker recess 'll come. I think recess is the nicest part of studying, don't you?"

"Yes," answered Steenie, with conviction. "Why, look there! There 's my Sutro talking to your father! And they 're walking away toward — oh! — do — you b'lieve they 'll go to the horse fields without us?"

"I s'pose they will."

"Oh, dear!"

At which tone of regret, Beatrice said, kindly, "You 're the queerest girl! But I 'll ask Papa to let us go, recess-time. Papa! Papa!"

The Judge turned about and waited while the children ran up to him. "Well, little folks! What now? How could you tear yourselves away from your dear books? Eh?"

"Now, Papa, please don't tease! I 'm sure you would n't like to have a whole line of hard, two-syllabled words to learn, and rows and rows of dazzly figures to add up, would you ?"

"I certainly should not; on such a morning as this, too. But if I were a little girl, two little girls, I'd go at those words and figures 'slap bang!' And I'd get them all tucked away inside of my cranium, so tight and sure that Ma'amselle would be obliged to say: 'Really, young ladies, *tres bien!* and I will compensate you for your so hard labor, and give you leave at eleven of the clock, precisely, to go to the library of the father and look in.'"

"And, what then ? What then, Papa?"

"Maybe, peanuts; maybe, horses. Different tastes need different rewards."

To Steenie this was not as intelligible as to Beatrice, who readily translated for her new friend's benefit Judge Courtenay's meaning, which was: that he evidently wished to be let alone then; but that if they were studious they might leave off lessons at eleven o'clock, and come to the library, when he would take them to see the horses. "If anybody cares about those old things!"

Steenie cared so very much that she infected Beatrice with her own feeling; and her few weeks at a "really school" had been of such use to her, that once her books were opened, she allowed herself no respite till she had conquered the tasks set before her.

Which good example was, also, infectious to the untrained Beatrice, who surprised and pleased Ma'amselle by her sudden attention to duty.

It is true that bright glances were occasionally darted back and forth, and signs exchanged to mark the progress of learning on either side ; but, in spite of this, when eleven o'clock came they not only had done their work with satisfaction to their teacher, but with real pleasure to themselves, — a cause of considerable astonishment, also.

"Now, for Papa and fun ! My father's a awful jolly man.   You can't 'most gen'ally tell if he's teasing or earnest.   But — he's nice."

" So's mine.   I guess fathers are always nice, are n't they ? "

." No, not always.   I know a father 'at whips his girl.   With a whip, like you do horses," asserted Beatrice, gravely.

" I never — whip horses !   Never !   I would n't be so cruel ! "

" My — sake !   Why, are you ' mad ? '   Why should n't you whip 'em ?   Everybody does."

"They don't at Santa Felisa. I've seen folks do it here, though; till I've had to run away an' cry. I think it's puf-fect-ly dreadful!"

"Why, Steenie Calthorp! You are the veriest oddest one! My Papa'll laugh at you. Pshaw! He whips horses himself; an' he's a Judge, — a Judge-of-the-Supreme-Court! If you know what that is."

"I don't. And I don't care if he is, he ought n't to. Bob says so, an' Bob knows. He says it's ruiny to any poor thing to do it. Once he caught a vaquero doing it to one of the Plun-ketty man's ploughers; and he just snatched the rawhide out of the fellow's hand, and gave it to the fellow himself! Just as he was hurting the horse. I tell you, was n't he mad? And did n't he jump around lively?"

"I should s'pose he did."

"And Bob says: 'Now you know how 't is yourself!' and that vaquero could be trusted any-where after that. Only once he tried to shoot Bob; so Bob had to lick him again, an' — that settled it."

"I should s'pose it did!" quoted an amused voice, and Judge Courtenay's hand rested lightly on Steenie's curly head. "You see I was tired waiting for eleven o'clock, because that old señor

of yours has promised me a treat, too; so I came
out to meet you on the path from your summer-
house school-room."

"How nice!   What is it, Papa?"

"This little girl is to give it to me."

"I?   Why, what can a little girl like me do
for a big man like you?" asked Steenie, in eager
wonder.

"Show me how Kentucky Bob tackles an
unbroken colt."

An instant's critical scrutiny of the genial face
before her convinced Steenie that the words were
"earnest," not "fun;" still — she could hardly
believe her own vision.   "Do you really, truly
mean it?"

"I really, truly do.   If you are not afraid."

"Afraid?   My!   I could n't be afraid of a
horse, could I?   I love them so; and my father
says that they know it, 'stinctively."

"Instinctively.   Well — the old caballero's
stories seem almost incredible; but now is your
chance to prove them true," responded Diablo's
owner, studying, in his turn, very critically the
animated face of the little girl beside him.   He
did not at all believe any of the "yarns" which
Sutro had- "spun" to him during their ramble
over the horse-farm; but he had immensely

enjoyed the boastful eloquence of one whom he considered a "crack-brained old man;" and he did not seriously intend allowing Steenie to approach nearer than a safe distance of the beautiful colt with the unsubdued will. But he thought it would give her a pleasure to watch Diablo over the paling; and he anticipated great amusement, also, in watching Vives "back down" when once brought face to face with fact, — fact in the shape of a "vicious" four-year-old whom the best horse-trainers had, as yet, been unable to reduce to submission.

But he had n't counted at all upon the perfect honesty and credulity of "the Little Lady of the Horse," nor her own proud acceptance of the title which her adoring Santa Felisans had given their "Little Un;" else what followed then would never have happened.

As they came to the paddock, and looked over the paling, Diablo's owner pointed him out as: "The handsome brute! There he is. As powerful and wicked as his name denotes. Locked up in those shapely limbs is a mint of money, — that nobody dares conquer for me. A fine animal, eh?"

"He's perfect! Oh, you beauty, you darling!"

Diablo stood at the extreme end of his paddock, head up, eyes flashing, every nerve quivering at sound of human voices. Of late, many attempts had been made to "break him;" each resulting in fresh torment to himself, and failure to his would-be conquerors. Already he had learned to distrust humanity, and to watch against its assaults.

"Your lariat, Sutro," whispered Steenie, eagerly. And from his capacious pocket the caballero drew a fine silken cord which he always carried, and silently gave it to her.

The Judge's attention had been diverted, for an instant, but was recalled by a swish of flying draperies, and Beatrice's low cry: "My — sake!"

Steenie had leaped over the fence, and was swiftly proceeding down the field, with the springing step of one who merrily goes to meet a friend.

"Merciful powers! Steen —"

But Sutro's hand was firmly placed over Judge Courtenay's lips. "Ten thousand pardons! Speak not — move not. Her safety and success depend on silence," whispered the caballero, impressively.

"Her success!" Strong man though he was, Diablo's owner turned faint, and he shut his eyes in horror at this terrible result of his own idle jesting.

CHAPTER X.

OWEVER, the Judge quickly aroused from the inaction his terror had caused, and, leaping over the paling, would have followed this childish horse "breaker," had he been allowed. But Sutro sprang forward almost as instantly,

STEENIE, DIABLO, AND THE JUDGE.

leaned over the rails, and, with all the force of his iron muscles, clasped his long arms around the other's shoulders.

"*Caramba!* I tell thee — no! Thou shalt not! Wouldst see her killed before thy very eyes?"

In a whisper, equally hoarse, the pinioned victim of the Spaniard's embrace retorted: "No! For that reason — "

"Move not, hand nor foot! Watch. She is safe. I swear it. She has a magic. I know not — she calls it love."

Magic! It seemed so. Half way down the field Steenie slackened her pace, began to sing softly, bits and snatches of melodies ended almost in the same breath, and to stop and pluck at the buttercup and clover blooms, here or there. She had the lariat loosely about her wrist; but she paid no attention to Diablo, who stood, like a beautiful statue, regarding the intrusion.

By slow degrees she made her way to a low-branched oak-tree standing at one side the paddock, not far from the colt's own position, and, with the gentlest of motions, raised herself to its broad limb.

Diablo was now obliged to turn his head in order to watch her, but otherwise he did not stir; and, observing this, Judge Courtenay's heart beat a trifle more naturally.

"Loose your arms, señor; I shall not startle her now."

"Ah! *Si?* Thou beholdest then that we spoke the truth? In one half-hour my Little Un will come to thee leading the beast by the forelock. Thou wilt see."

"Hang the beast! That she comes out alive — unhurt — is all I care!"

"In verity she will. do that. She will do a miracle. Thou shalt see."

"Is it possible that you are not afraid? I thought you called her your 'heart's dearest'!"

"*En verdad.* She is the whole world to Sutro Vives. But I am not afraid, I. She is all love, all innocence, all fearlessness. She would win over the Evil One himself, I believe, if she could meet him!"

"She certainly has a chance now to try!" groaned Diablo's owner, too anxious to be greatly amused by Sutro's extravagance of language, and holding himself ready to rush forward to the child's aid at the first ugly movement on the animal's part.

Timid Beatrice stood upon the lower round of the fence, scarcely breathing in the fascination of her fear; yet it was her eyes which interpreted the first overture between those two out there in the paddock. "See! She's laid her head down on the branch an' pertends she's going to sleep; and I can hear her — I surely can — singing soft, soft, kind of loving-y like. And now — he's moving — but slow — as anything."

"Yes. I am watching." Neither voice raised above a whisper.

"But — look now! He's a walking up to her; curious like, is n't he? He's — see him!"

Intently they gazed upon the pantomime.

Steenie lay on her leafy perch, one little foot dangling and swinging lazily back and forth, her blue eyes turned caressingly, almost imploringly, upon Diablo, as if beseeching him to come to her.

Her own description, afterward, was: " I just thought *at* him as hard as ever I could. I would n't think of anything else, only that I did love him, and was sorry he did n't make friends with his wanted-to-be friends, and I wanted he should know 'bout it. And by-and-by, I s'pose my thought hit his somewhere, — as Bob believes, — and then — it was done. He just came closer an' closer; an' by-an'-by he stretched out his pretty nose and smelled of my foot. Then he waited a minute, an' I did n't even wink, but just kept on saying, inside of me: 'Don't you see I love you? Don't you know I love you?'

" Pretty soon he sniffed at my hand in my lap; and then he ate the clover blossoms; an' then he let me move one finger a little bit — though he jumped at that. Afterwards, I could move my whole hand, and smooth his face, that was soft as satin. When I could coax his head down to mine, so I could talk into his ears, I had no more to do. I remembered everything Bob taught me; and when I knew he was all right, and was n't afraid any more, I let him smell of the lariat, and fuss with it 's long as he liked. Then I made a slip-halter, — Bob's way, — an' that 's all.''

That was all, perhaps, but it was marvellous in Judge Courtenay's eyes ; while those of old Sutro shone with fond pride.

" I told thee so, señor! See — she is leading him as gentle as a lamb. Come, little señorita, let us move back a space, and leave him to be presented to one at a time. The master first, as is right it should be.''

" Well! " ejaculated that gentleman, left in the paddock, regarding with growing astonishment the small figure which approached, leading Diablo by his silken thrall, and with one arm thrown upward upon his neck. " You are the most wonderful child in the United States ! "

Steenie smiled, and her eyes shone, but not from vanity at this unbounded praise. She had been hearing just such exclamations all her life from her beloved, outspoken Santa Felisans, and she knew that they came only from a mutual love. But she was proud of her new conquest; and she led Diablo close to his master, and held out the end of the cord for the Judge to take. "If you are just gentle with him, sir, he 'll behave beautifully. He 's been frightened; that 's all."

He was frightened still, and, at the first motion of his owner's extended hand, drew backward, nervously.

" Frightened! If ever I saw ugliness in a brute, I see it in him now. Observe his eyes."

" Oh, don't say that, sir, please! You don't understand. 'Xcuse me, but I 'm sure you don't. Bob says a fine horse is all ' nerves,' an' the ' most sensitive thing in creation.' He says folks ought to treat 'em like babies; 'cause they feel things more. Softly, my pretty one! Don't you be afraid. Steenie 'll let nobody hurt you — not a body —even him! "

" Hm-m! "

" Somebody 's whipped him sometime, or struck him cruelly."

" Why should n't they? He 's acted like a villain."

" I wish I 'd been here! He would n't then — 'cause I know. See. He 's all gentle now. You may put your hand on his nose; but it must be kind — kind — 'cause that 's the way."

Diablo did permit his master to fondle him; and at the first touch of the delicate nostrils all the Judge's love for horse-flesh sprang to the front, and with it a subtler appreciation of horse-nature than he had ever before known. "Poor fellow! Is it so? Are you not really vicious? — then I'll not part with you."

"Part with him? Why, sir?"

"Because I thought he would be useless to us. I bought him for a carriage horse, to match that other colt, Brown Bess; but, while she is breaking in like a kitten, he has resisted everybody. I think he will again — after you go away from him."

"Then I won't go away. Oh, wait a moment! I've thought of something. S'posin' you teach Diablo to be your very own, ownest horse; s'posin' you don't let any grooms or anybody do anything for him but just you, yourself! You could make him as smart as Tito, maybe."

"'Maybe'? Is Tito so brilliant, then?" asked the Judge, smiling, and greatly delighted that Diablo now stood quietly beside them, nibbling at the grass or sniffing about Steenie's curly head, without resenting their presence or voices. Sutro and Beatrice had also drawn near and leaned against the paling to hear what the others were saying.

"Why — he doesn't — shine. That's 'brilliant,' isn't it? But he's awful 'telligy — I mean intelligent. Bob says, 'He's the brainiest horse he's 'quainted with, an' sweetest tempered to boot.' He knows every single word I say to him; and if he can't talk much with his tongue, he does with his actions an' his eyes. He drives without reins, an' he waltzes — beau-u-tifully! An' he limps, an' 'goes it blind,' an' does the cutestest things you ever saw a horse do. Oh, won't you let Diablo be just as clever? Either for your own self or Beatrice? Would n't you like Diablo for your very own, Beatrice?"

"No; I should not," answered that young person, decisively.

"I've half a mind to try your notion, little one! There's no fool like an old fool, they say; and, maybe, I shall do better at horse-training than at law. It's a step upwards, too, from the 'bench' to the saddle! But — I confess I'm very ignorant. The 'breaking' of my horses has always been left to professional trainers. I have, heretofore, been perfectly satisfied to accept results only."

"It seems perfectly funny to hear 'bout 'breaking' horses like they were dishes. Bob says it's a wrong word, an' it's 'sponsible for more suffering to the poor things 'an any other word in the language."

"Humph! Who is this oracle, 'Bob'?"

Steenie explained, and the Judge was so interested that he exclaimed: "I wonder if I could n't
induce him to come out here and take care of
my stock-farm?"

"Maybe," answered Steenie; "but I don't
guess so. He says there is n't room enough for
his lungs out East. He needs a great deal of
breathin' space."

"Well — Bob or no Bob — will you give an
old man like me a few lessons in horse-break —
What word shall I use?"

"It's teaching, — just teaching 'em. Like
Beatrice an' I go to school. It's funny for me
to tell you things, is n't it? 'Cause my grandmother thinks you 're a — what did she call it!
A very wonderful magician — no, lo-gician; and
when I asked her what that was, she said maybe
I could understand 'smart' better."

"Thank you. Now, when shall our next
lesson be?"

"To-morrow — to-morrow — that ever is. 'Cause
it does n't do to let Diablo forget us. He's same
as babies yet. He has n't learned to remember."

"To-morrow, then; and I am greatly indebted
to you. I believe — with both halves of my
mind, now — I will decide to act wholly upon

your suggestion, and see what comes of it. I
will train him for myself, alone. I shall be at
home, hereafter, for some weeks; and the opportunity is mine."

"Oh, how glad I am! Do you hear that,
Diablo, darling? You're going to be nobody's
horse but just this kind, kind man's! You're
never to be whipped, nor loaded, nor over-driven,
nor checked-back, nor strapped-down, nor anything horrid like these queer Old Knollsboro
folks do to horses!"

"Hold on, hold on! I have not promised any
of these 'thousand and one' things, little lady!
I shall want him to be useful."

"Of course, and that's why you won't do
them. I saw some poor horses on the street
yesterday. They were before a big carriage, as
heavy, as heavy! And they had ugly straps to
hold their poor heads up — this way! Till their
throats ached so they couldn't breathe, hardly.
Not like you help them with a strap when they're
racing, so the wind won't choke in their 'pipes,' —
'cause that isn't bad, just for the little minute
they have 'em so; but these were all crooked
back, terr'ble, so they couldn't see, only a
little way up toward the sky. They had a
mis'able action; 'cause they had 'blinders' on,

besides, and all they dared to do was just step straight up an' down, up an' down, fear they'd hurt themselves.   The coachman was lashing them to make them go, — 'cause his carriage folks seemed in a hurry; an' I should have laughed at him, if I had n't had to cry for them — the horses.   I could n't help thinking 'bout 'em when I went to bed; an' my father says 'It's ign'rant cruelty,' an' 'if the folks understood horses' feelings, like they'd ought to, why everybody'd be gladder.'"

"Humph!   You're a very close observer.   And now, shall I lift you over the fence?"

"No, thank you.   I'm going to walk once around the paddock with Diablo, and 'xplain to him 'bout our having to go, and our coming back to-morrow, an' everything.   You can bid him good-by, if you want to."

"May I, indeed?   How shall I do it?"

"Why — same's folks.   Same's me.   Say, 'Good-morning, Diablo; pleased to make your 'quaintance,' or anything nicey sounding an' p'lite.   He knows, Diablo does.   An' you want him brought up like a gentleman's horse, don't you?   So he'll understand when folks use good language, an' not what Papa calls 'ruffian talk.' He knows, Diablo does.   See here?   See that

fine head, broad as anything above the eyes?
That's 'cause it's full of brains; an' brains are
where folks think an' know things. If he had n't
have had a good head, he would n't have understood me so soon, first off. He looks as if he
might be as clever as Tito, 'most."

"Good-morning, Diablo. I am sincerely delighted to make friends with you," said Judge
Courtenay, very gravely, though with a twinkle
in his eyes.

But Steenie did not care for the twinkle, only
laughed in return; and, by her hand upon his
face forcing the colt's head down, she gently
grasped his forelock and bent it still lower.
"Bow p'litely, dear Diablo, 'cause you'd ought
to." Then she walked away as she had come,
with her arm upon his shoulder, and his light
leading-string held carelessly in her other hand.

The Judge climbed back over the paling, and,
catching sight of Sutro's exultant face, laughed
and pulled out his watch. "Well, old fellow!
You're a pretty good prophet! Five minutes
past time, that's all."

"*Caramba!* More than that since she brought
him up to thee with the lariat round his nozzle,
no?"

"Beaten — beaten! I give it up. But do you

know, señor, that you have the honor to serve a
very remarkable young person?"

"Ten thousand pardons, Señor Juez [Judge], I
have known that forever. *Si.*"

"Hm-m. There she comes; and I leave it to
you, Señor Vives, to convey to her family my
acknowledgment of her services. If in any way
I can serve her or them, they have but to command me."

The Judge had a better understanding of
human than equine nature. He knew that he
could not have found a messenger more delighted
to carry messages of courtesy than old Sutro, nor
one who would do so more gracefully. He knew,
also, that his cordial gratitude would be shorn of
nothing, but rather embellished, by its passage
over the caballero's lips.

"At thy feet, señor. Thy appreciation of our
so beloved one will give pleasure to our household. I have the honor to salute thee; and—
Service? Ten thousand pardons—but there is
a way in which—at thy leisure—"

Again the Judge pulled out his watch. "You
have but to name, as I said. To-morrow, during
the children's study-hour, I will be pleased to
hear your suggestions."

"Thanks. Thanks. The service old Sutro

claims is for our ' Little Lady of the Horse,' —
not for himself. *Mañana*, then ; and *Adios!* "

Five minutes later, Steenie, mounted upon her
Tito, and with her caballero walking proudly by
her side, paced slowly out of the Judge's grounds.
"It has been a good, good day, my Sutro! Such
a happiness! You will be happy too, is it not?
And what do you think, besides? That kind,
splendid gentleman says that he has a pretty,
black horse, whom nobody uses much, that shall
be loaned to you whenever we wish for a long
ride. Then you will not have to go hobblety-bob
on those poor worn-out livery hacks. Are you
not glad?"

"Glad. *En verdad.* But of more yet, *mi niña.*
Old Sutro has something in his head besides nonsense, no? Listen. He offered service — and
there is a way, in verity. I told him. *Mañana*
— he will do it, and Sutro's heart will be at
peace. Thou wilt then have money — more
than thou canst ever use. It is so. I tell thee."

"Su-tro-Vi-ves! What — have you done?
Have you asked that gentleman for money? Do
you need it? Why not ask my father, then?
Oh, Sutro!"

"*Tente* [hold on]! Thou leapest to a blunder
as Tito does over a hurdle. I have asked no

man for money, I. Why not? Because, in all
California, there is no man who has more of it
than I. And what I have I will give to thee.
Thou art to be my *heredera* [heiress], thou. After
Sutro Vives thou wilt inherit."

"Ah! ha, ha, my rich one! And what shall
I inherit, sir? All your whims and notions, and
your old sombrero, maybe? 'No?'"

"'*Sta buen*'! Laugh if thou wilt; in derision
now, but, by-and-by, in glee. And what shalt
thou inherit? Wait and see. Wait and see. I
would have told thee but for thy ridicule. No
matter. Quite time enough for thee — when
Sutro Vives is done with life. Which will be
soon, no? But I say — yes."

"And I say no, no, no! good Sutro," said
Steenie, sobered instantly by the gloomy look
which settled upon her old comrade's face. "You
are to live longer than any Vives who ever was,
and to use every bit of your wonderful riches for
your own cristy, crusty, blessed self. Hear me
say that, my caballero, — I, your own 'Little Lady
of the Horse'! So there! And home again!"

Sutro smiled once more. His mood was wholly
dependent upon that of his beloved "*niña's*," who
was his one object in life; and, with the smile
still upon his face, he swung her from Tito's back,

and led the latter away to the comfortable stall which now bade fair to become his permanent home.

"Here we are, Papa, Grandmother! And the loveliest time in all the world! Oh, it's just fun, fun, fun to go to school in a summer-house — and be a colt teacher afterward — Why, Papa! What — what is the matter? Are your eyes —"

But she did not finish the sentence. A groan, such as is wrung from strong men only by great trouble, fell from her father's lips, as he stretched out his arms to enfold her, and dropped his poor, sightless eyes upon her shoulder. "My dear little Steenie! What is to become of you!"

The child's glance flew round to her grandmother's face; but its expression startled her even more than her father's despondency. Madam Calthorp sat gazing straight before her, but seeing nothing, saying nothing, while every drop of blood seemed to have left her white cheek, and the seams of an added decade to have fallen upon it.

"Grandmother — don't! Don't look like that! What awful thing has happened? Do speak to me — please! Somebody!"

The words broke the spell of that strange

silence. But Steenie had never in her life seen anything so sorrowful as the gaze which came out of vacancy to fix itself upon her own person.

"My poor little darling, everything has come upon us — but death. We are ruined. Ruined!"

CHAPTER XI.

NOBODY said anything more.

Steenie stood perfectly still, too perplexed to even try to understand what "ruin" meant; till, after awhile, her father lifted his head and released her from this, to her terrible, position. Then she darted from

RESOLVED TUBBS.

the room and from those tragic faces, as if, by turning her back upon them, she could banish them from her thought.

In the kitchen she found Resolved Tubbs with his Bible on his knee.

Now Resolved was a good man, a really sincere Christian; but Steenie had lived long enough in the house to learn that when Brother Tubbs sat down at midday with his Bible on his knee and his spectacles pulled into place, he was in a state of mind to read Jeremiah only, and ignore the more joyful prophets.

She had come with the gayest of spirits into the astonishing gloom of the household, and she wanted no more dismalness; so she tarried in the kitchen but long enough to catch one sepulchral gleam from Resolved's uplifted "glasses," and passed out into the garden where she had seen Mary Jane calmly gathering strawberries.

"Well, it can't be so awful, I believe, or she would n't be doing that!" thought the troubled child, and hurried forward to the housekeeper's side.

"Mary Jane! dear Mary Jane! Whatever has happened? What is 'ruin,' and who has done it?"

"Hm-m. That's a'most more'n I can say. Did n't they tell ye nothin', dearie?"

"Not a thing. Only Papa says: 'What's to become of me!' and Grandmother: 'We 're ruined.' But I think Mr. Resolved knows, 'cause he's sitting down an' looking unhappy reading. What is it?"

"The miser'ble unbeliever! — even if he is my

own flesh an' blood! Why can't he turn to an' do sunthin', an' keep a-thinkin': 'The Lord 'll provide,' stidder huntin' out more trouble from the blessed Book? I've a mind ter go in an' shake him!"

"Why, Mary Jane! Shake Mr. Tubbs!" Steenie's horrified imagination picturing that lumbago-tortured old man in his sister's vigorous grasp.

"Well, o' course, not really. But, I'd like ter know! Here comes the bad news, an' down flops the hull fambly, an' goes ter sighin' — furnaces! Stidder ary one liftin' finger ter see what kin be done 'bout it. That ain't my way o' 'terpretin' the Scripters; an' I don't want it ter be your'n."

"I guess it won't be, Mary Jane. I don't like to feel bad, never."

"No more do I! So — reckin you 'll be as well off out here 'ith me, doin' sunthin', as anywheres elset, fer the space o' the next short time. So — jest set down on the grass there, dearie, an' hull what berries I've got picked, while I get some more; an' I 'll tell yer all I know 'bout anything."

Steenie promptly obeyed. Mary Jane's cheerfulness of temper was very pleasant, and they had long ago become fast friends. " Now — tell, please."

" Hm-m. Plain's I understand it, it's this way : Your pa an' yer granma has lost every dollar they had in the world. They're as poor now as I be, — poorer."

" Well ? " asked Steenie, to whom " dollars " and " poverty " conveyed no distinct impression.

" Well ?   Ain't that enough ?   But I don't b'lieve you re'lize it a mite. I can't, hardly myself yet, nuther. But all the money yer granma had, an' it wa'n't more 'n jest enough ter keep us livin', plain an' comfort'ble as we do, was up in a bank, some'res. I hain't no faith in banks. They're 'tarnally bu'stin', er doin' sunthin' startlin'. I always keep mine in a stockin' ; an' the stockin' 's in a big blue box in the bottom o' that hair trunk o' mine. Things bein' so uncertain in this life, I think it's best ter tell ye ; but don't ye lisp a word, — not even to brother Resolved. 'Cause he'd be boun' ter have it put in some differ'nt place not half so safe. In case I should be took off suddent, as folks sometimes is, somebody'd oughter know ; an' you're trustible. I've found that out."

" Thank you. But, about the bank. What is it ? "

" Beat if I kin tell ye plain. 'Cause I don't scurce know myself. Old Knollsboro bank is that big brick buildin' acrost from the stun churcn. An' in it, somehow, folks hides all the money they have ; an' the bank folks pays 'em out little dribs on 't to a time ; an' that 's all they have ter keep house on. That 's as near as I kin put it. Most every town has a bank, too ; but, 'cause yer pa thought they was n't no other so safe as the old one here to Knollsboro he uset ter put all his sellery, too, inter this one ; an' now it 's done jest like the rest on 'em often does, — it 's bu'sted. That 's what Resolved calls it. Yer granma said ' failed ; ' but I 'low it comes ter the same thing when it means 'at every dollar they had, uther one, is lost, somehow. An' what 's wusser: yer granma owned ' stawk ' in it, too ; though how anybody could keep a livin' head er critter an' not never let it be seen, 's more 'n I fathom er try ter. I s'pose they par- tered it out, er sunthin.' An' now that stawk 's gone too, an' ter make it good, she 's li'ble ter a hull lot o' thousan' dollars. Think on it ! Ever so many hull — 'durin' — thousan' — dollars ! An she says — I heered her tellin' Mr. Dan'l — that ' she must pay it if it took this house.' An' he says : ' Mother ! Where you 've lived yer

hull life! It would kill you!' — an' I 'low it
would."

"But how could a body pay anything with a
house?"

"Sell it, I s'pose, an' take that money an' throw
it arter t'other 'at 's gone. I dunno, rightly; fer
that 's jest what I asted Resolved, an' all he said
was: 'Sil-ly women! Sell er mortgage — sil-ly
wom-en! They don't never have no heads fer
business!' So, arter that, I knowed no more 'n
I did afore, — which was n't nothin', square. But
how 's a body to l'arn if their men critters won't
l'arn 'em? An' I guess we 've got as many
berries as we shall eat ter-day; an' that 's
knowledge more in my line 'n tryin' ter explain
things I don't understan'. So let 's go in out o'
the sun."

They entered the house, whither Sutro had pre-
ceded them, and found that sociable person vainly
endeavoring to extract more than monosyllables
from the lips of his house-mate, Tubbs. At
which Mary Jane's ready wrath burst forth upon
her pessimistic brother.

"I don't see what ails you — Resolved, 'at ye
can't give a body a civil answer! You — hain't
lost nothin', 'at I knows on. An' if ye call it a
Christian way o' meetin' trials, ter set there an'

let a poor heathen Mexicer pester the life out on ye 'fore ye 'll speak him a decent word, I dunno! It ain't the way with good Baptist folks, anyhow."

As Mr. Tubbs had long before accepted the Methodist creed, while his sister had professed another, this was an old bone of contention, which he was quite ready to pick up, to the forgetfulness of newer grievances.

Which was exactly what Mary Jane desired. " Best way ter stir Resolved out o' the hypoes is ter make him mad! Then he 'll fly 'round an' fergit lumbago an' ever'thing elset. He 'll chop more kindlin' in ten minutes when he 's riled, 'an he will in a hull day when things goes ter suit him."

He became " riled " on the instant, and shut his Bible with a bang, while his spectacles were shoved into their usual resting-place upon his bald head with an energy that endangered the glass.

To escape an impending war of words, Steenie retreated to the presence of her own kin once more, and this time with a determination to beg from them enough information to enable her to understand clearly this new anxiety they were suffering.

" Yes, Steenie, I will tell you," said Madam

Calthorp, gently, and quite in her natural manner again. "But do you go out of doors, Daniel.
The air is better for you, and Sutro has returned.
I will be careful in my disclosures, but there is no
need for you to hear the painful repetition."

Mr. Calthorp rose wearily. There was a look
of hopelessness about his fine face which even
blindness had not brought to it; and Steenie
watched him depart with a heavier heart than
she had ever known.

"Now, Grandmother."

"Yes, dear. To begin with, though we were
never rich, neither were we poor. We had
enough, with economy, to provide for all our
ordinary needs, and a surplus for emergencies.
What your father had inherited and acquired,
together with my own money, was all in one
place, — intrusted to a corporation of which your
grandfather was the founder, and which people
said was 'as good as the bank of England.'
Some weeks ago, about the time you came from
Santa Felisa, I heard rumors of trouble about
this money of ours, and I instituted inquiries to
verify or disprove them. The report brought to
me was that they were without foundation,
that our possessions were as secure as they had
always seemed, and that I need have no uneasi-

ness whatever. I did not mention these rumors to my son, because his own personal affliction appeared to be as much as he — as any of us — could bear; but now I wish that I had done so. Of course he could not read; and his sensitiveness about meeting people, together with my mistaken kindness, kept him wholly ignorant until the blow fell. This morning, after you left us, a messenger was sent to us by the directors, announcing the sudden and utter failure of the bank; as well as that I, a stockholder, am liable — that is, in debt — for several thousand dollars. Now, this is exactly our situation: I own this house and a small farm in another part of the county. That I can sell for enough to pay my indebtedness, except about one thousand dollars. Many poor people will be losers by this failure, and I cannot rest, retaining anything — even if I might — which would relieve their necessities. So, the only course left us is to sell this house also; and out of its proceeds pay the extra one thousand. There will be a small sum remaining, or should be, — enough I hope to hire a tiny cottage somewhere; but how we are to exist in that cottage the future alone can prove."

Steenie listened attentively, breathlessly; her

big blue eyes fixed upon her grandmother's face, and rejoicing in the calmness which had returned to it. She did not know that the only expression of distress which the proud Madam had given, had been the one exclamation at first sight of her own self. " Everything has come upon us — but death. We are ruined. Ruined ! "

" When, Grandmother ? When will we go to the cottage ? "

" Oh, I do not know. Not just yet. The adjustment of these matters will take time; we shall not be disturbed in the immediate present; but the eventual condition of affairs will be what I have decided already. And Steenie, my dear little child, now you have a chance to be even doubly helpful to your poor father. Blindness is a trial which no seeing person can comprehend ; but for a strong man to suffer it, and to know that he cannot do one thing to alleviate the necessities of those who are dear to him, is terrible. It is this which is so intolerable to my son. If he could regain his sight, no matter how poor he was, he would face the world gayly for your sake and mine. He would work for us and forget all the mishap; but to be idle in such a strait — ah ! I know from my own heart what it must be to him."

"Poor, poor papa! But can't *I* do something? Maybe I can! I'm not blind nor old, and I'm as strong as strong. See here! I can lift a chair ever so high! And Judge Courtenay says I'm most puffectly 'veloped for a ten-year-old goin' on 'leven. I'm much bigger 'n Beatrice, an' she's half-past twelve. Is n't there some way, Grandmother, dear Grandmother? Think, please; in that in-telligence of yours, maybe you'll find out something. And if you do — won't I do it! Just you see!"

"You precious baby! If your ability only matched your courage, Grandmother knows that you would banish every care from all our hearts! But, yes; there is one thing you can do: bear whatever deprivations you may have with that same sunny spirit; be patient when, by-and-by, we older folks begin to lose our own serenity, and grow fretful, perhaps, and difficult to get along with. You can remember then that it is n't what you call our 'truly selves,' but the worn nerves and depressed hearts that cause the sharp words and moods. Early to learn a woman's lesson, my gay little Steenie; but I believe you are capable of learning it well."

All which Steenie did not quite understand. This book-loving old student was apt to " talk

over the head" of a "'most-'leven"-year-old; but
she gained this much: that, no matter what happened, she was to make things as bright as she
could, and her loving heart responded loyally.

"I'll be as patient as patient. And I'll never
let my papa think a thing I can help; and —
Oh! There's the dinner-bell!"

Probably this common, every-day sound was a
relief to everybody in the house; and though the
meal was served a full hour later than usual, the
extra care which had been expended upon it more
than compensated for the delay.

"Oh, Mary Jane! How good that beefsteak·
does smell!"

"Humph! Better enjoy it while ye kin. Only
the Lord knows how long any on us 'll eat beefsteak!" commented Resolved Tubbs, dolefully.

"Hush yer complainin', can't ye! An' as long
as the Lord continners ter bother 'ith us poor
worms an' sends porter-houses, receive 'em in the
same sperrit, an' be thankful!" retorted Mary
Jane.

"Well, I call that sacrilegious, if you have
enj'yed full immersion!" said the brother, snap-
ping at a fly upon the table-cloth with such energy
as to upset the salt.

"There it goes! Only the quer'l come afore

the upsettin'. An' I do say it : I'd ruther be
sacrilegious with my tongue, 'an so sack-cloth-an'-
ashesy with my sperrit."

"Resolved! Mary Jane!" remonstrated Madam, sternly, yet with a smile dawning upon
her lips. And if ever a quarrel can be said to be
opportune, that one was ; for Steenie laughed
outright, and Sutro tittered, while even Mr. Calthorp lost the gravity of his expression for a little.

It was a good dinner! And there was more
sense in Mary Jane's philosophy than in her
brother's after all; for the savory dishes tempted
appetites into existence, and through material
enjoyment made even mental disquietude easier
to endure.

But after dinner was over, Mr. Calthorp retired
to his own room and closed the door, and Madam
retreated to her library; so that Steenie, driven
to her own resources, did the most natural thing
in the world : got Sutro to saddle Tito and set
off for a gallop, leaving the old caballero to attend upon her father, "case he should come out
an' want somebody an' not both of us be gone."

Sutro remained, partly on account of Steenie's
argument, and partly that for a long ride he
utterly disdained the livery hack it had been his
fortune to use during his stay at Old Knollsboro ;

for he did not feel quite free to go to Rookwood, so soon again, and borrow "the pretty black horse" which had been offered for his enjoyment.

Thus he was forced to hear various unpleasant remarks from Resolved Tubbs' grim lips about "plenty o' mouths ter fill 'ithout no furriners," and so on; all which, busied in visions of his own brain, he ignored as referring to himself. For was n't he at that very moment planning the details of a scheme which should enrich everybody?

As for Steenie, she gave Tito his head, and he took it, far out into the open country, with a will and spirit that drove every care from his little rider's mind. But after he had travelled a long distance he cast a shoe; and, seeing a smithy near, Steenie rode up to the door and coolly requested to have the shoe set.

"Humph! Who are you, any way, child? And who is going to pay me for my trouble?" demanded the farrier, with equal coolness.

Pay for it? Why, at Santa Felisa, the smith was "their own" — nobody paid. Here — Steenie did n't like such difficult questions, but she answered, simply enough: "I s'pose somebody will. I 'm Steenie Calthorp; and Tito can't

go home barefoot, over these rough roads, can
he ? You must see that for yourself, Mr. Smith,
don't you ? "

" I see that, plain enough ; and if you are one
of the Calthorps down at Knollsboro — here
goes ! They 're honest folks, and always have
been. Never a poor man lost a cent by them,
and that 's the truth. They 're the right kind of
aristocrats, they are. Pay for what they have,
and what they can't pay for go without, and no
complaining. But no matter this time aboot
pay for a trifle of kindness like this. I 'll
shoe this handsome fellow, and proud of the
job, any time you choose to ride out this way
and show me how a little girl *can* ride when
she puts her mind to it. That 's so. You may
count upon it."

" Why, Mr. Smith ! I 'm sure that 's very kind
of you, an' I 'preciate it. I like to see a man
shoe a horse, when he does it neatly, an' what
Bob calls ' with sense of a horse's feelings.' I
think I could almost be a farrier myself, sometimes. I do, so."

" A farrier, hey ? There 's something you
could do far better than that. Where did you
learn to ride ? "

" I never learned. I always rode."

" Where ? "

" At Santa Felisa, California."

" So ?   Then all I have to say is that you had better set up a school and teach some of these young folks round here, who almost murder their horses with their blundering clumsiness. For I never saw anybody sit a horse as well as you do ; and that's the truth."

When the shoe was set, Steenie thanked the helpful smith, promised to visit him again, and went on her way homeward.   But she was very thoughtful and preoccupied ; and Tito, fully sympathizing with her mood, dropped into a gentle canter, and broke his pleasant pace not once till his mistress suddenly bent forward and threw her arms around his neck.

" Tito, my Tito !   I 'll do it !   I will, I will ! "

Tito softly nodded up and down.   Whatever she meant to do, — and it was something which made her eyes shine and her face dimple with hopeful smiles, — be sure that her wise playfellow fully intended to help her.

CHAPTER XII.

WELL, Señor Vives, I am at your service now," announced Judge Courtenay, at the next appearance of Steenie and her caballero at Rookwood. " In what can I advise you?"

RATTLESNAKE.

"Hm-m. It is a profound secret. Ten thousand pardons, Señor Juez [Mr. Judge] ; but I may close the door, no?"

" Close it, certainly, if you wish; but we are not likely to be disturbed. This is my private office."

" I would not, for a hundred worlds that others should hear what I disclose!" repeated old Sutro, cautiously.

" You are perfectly safe. Be assured."

" *Si?* Then here is my desire: I wish to prepare my *testamento* [will]. In verity, that is

my hope and prayer." The Spaniard's face wore
an expression of grave importance.

"Your will? Well, that is, indeed, a serious
matter. Have you fully considered it?"

"*Caramba!* Have I not? *En verdad*, it has
long since been arranged — in here," said the
client, tapping his forehead, solemnly.

"Very well, then, let us to business. Give me
the points of the matter, and my clerk shall draw
up the paper."

"Clerk? No, no! No. *Por Dios!* No.
Thinkest thou that I would give such knowledge as I shall make known to the winds? It is
a secret, I tell thee. A secret!"

"Very well, then," answered the Judge, a
little impatiently. He was a very busy man,
just then enjoying a needed vacation, and he
had little inclination for clerical work, especially in a case like this where the interests at
stake were, presumably, very small. He was
doing what he did for Steenie's sake only;
because the old Californian was dear to the
child in whom he was so much interested.
"Very well, then; let us begin. What is the
first bequest?"

"The first? It is the last, — first, last, and
the whole. I wish to give everything I possess

— that is Santa Trinidad — to the most adorable Doña Steenie Calthorp."

"Indeed ? You are generous. What is Santa Trinidad ?"

"It is a mountain. It was part of Santa Felisa Rancho, when San' Felis' was greater than now, and belonged to the family of Vives, yes."

"It is valuable ?"

For a moment the eye of the old man gleamed craftily; then he asked: "Must thou know that ?"

"As you please."

Sutro considered. By nature he was not very secretive, and of lesser matters he was as sure to babble as to breathe ; but this was different. He held, or believed that he held, knowledge of utmost importance ; and he had seen enough of property dealings among the — to him — new possessors of his old California to understand that it was just the knowledge which would make them defraud him if they could. Lord Plunkett had seemed an honest man ; yet it was such as Lord Plunkett who had usurped the broad acres once belonging to his own race and people.   However, he must trust somebody. He must have help.

" *Caramba!* Wilt thou, Senor Juez, swear — *por Dios* — that thou wilt not betray me? That I can trust thee?"

"You can trust me entirely, but I will not swear; for I give my oath to no man," answered the Judge, becoming interested.

For a full half-minute Sutro stared fixedly into the face of his new friend; then, reading in that noble countenance nothing but good-will and uprightness, he plunged into his subject with a recklessness which hid nothing, either of knowledge or imagination. "La Trinidad is a cloven mountain. Its inhabitants are rattlesnakes, who, poor beasts, the Americans fear. Not so Spaniards and men of sense — not even Indians; a thousand times not so old Sutro. Why? Because I understand, can meet them without peril; and because *they are the guards to treasure untold.* No man knows it save Sutro Vives — and now thou; but the heart of La Trinidad is a heart of — " The testator rose from his chair, his face thrilled by excitement, and placing his lips to the Judge's ear, hissed one word therein.

"What is that you say?"

Sutro repeated the whisper.

"What! Man alive! Do you mean it? Do you know this to be true?"

"As I know that the sun shines now. *En verdad.*"

"What proof have you?"

"This." Sutro unfastened his buckskin vest, and opened a leathern bag which depended from his swarthy neck. "Believest thou now?"

"I believe what I see, always. But that this came from Santa Trinidad, how am I to know that?"

"Humph! A caballero may lie, yes; but not where he loves as I love Doña Steenie. Sawest thou ever a child like her? Eyes of such clear truthfulness? Lips so loving and so sweet? Face so bonny? Ways so — not-to-be-resisted? And heart so pure? No, a thousand times. She is one — alone. She is under the especial charge of Heaven. She is worth all — all. If the whole of California were mine I would give it her, and know it were well given. I would so, yes!" And warmed by his own theme, the old man left his chair and paced the room, gesturing eloquently, as is the custom of his race.

Judge Courtenay's interest increased; but, at that moment, it centred less in the bequest than in the beneficiary. "I agree with you, Señor Vives, that there is something ' not-to-be-resisted ' about this ' Little Lady of the Horse,' as you say you Westerners call her; but still I cannot help wondering how she has gained your devotion so entirely."

"How? Listen and thou shalt learn. When the good *Dios* sent her into this world Sutro Vives was a miserable old man, — even then. He had been wronged — wronged — wronged — till his heart was hard and bitter. He had lost faith in everything, below and above; and he kept Santa Trinidad in spite of everybody, — because its serpent-infested rocks were a menace to the world. From them he meant to take his revenge. He used to carry them, the snakes, down to the *hacienda*, and place them where they would do the most harm. It was the only joy left.

"One day — the day they buried the poor Señora Calthorp — he carried a creature bigger, more venomous than any other. He turned it loose on the threshold of Santa Felisa, and sat down to watch. By-and-by, a little thing, all soft and white, came creeping, creeping through the doorway, and spied the serpent, yes. It was pretty, too, and soft; but it was not white nor good. The wicked Sutro watched. Santa Maria watched also. The little fingers went out and touched the reptile, and the Mother of God

touched a wicked heart. In a second — before
the beautiful head of the serpent could rear itself
— *la criaturita* [the baby girl] was in the old
man's arms. Did she hate him, no? *Gracias
a Dios* [Thanks be to God]! — she folded her
own little arms about his neck and buried her
rose-leaf face against his ugly face; and the
demon of hate and murder left him. *Si!* That
is the tale."

It was a moving one. Judge Courtenay was
not the man to resist its influence; nor did he
ever thereafter doubt one assertion of Sutro
Vives where Steenie was concerned. The love
that is rooted in superstition is love that lasts.

"Well, I will draw up the document for you
as carefully as possible. But the inheritor is a
minor. She must have some one appointed to
act for her until lawfully able to act for herself; in case your demise occurs prior to that
time."

This suggestion had a legal sound about it that
captivated Sutro's ears; and he gathered enough
of its meaning to reply: "I understand. If I
die, it is the Señor Calthorp and Kentucky Bob
who will carry out my desires, no? But I do
not wish to die first. I wish to live, I myself."

"Yes — yes! We all wish that."

" And must I die that my little one may get the good of Santa Trinidad ? "

" There is nothing to prevent your giving it to her now, while you are still alive; but a ' last will and testament' implies the death of the testator before action is taken upon it." Then Judge Courtenay went on to explain, as simply and briefly as he could, the various methods by which Sutro Vives could benefit his favorite; and the old Spaniard did the best he could to comprehend.

But gradually a belief came into Sutro's mind, and fixed itself there, that if he died she would be better off. Because while he lived nobody would care to spend the necessary money to investigate the discovery he claimed, — mining being a most expensive business; but if he were dead, Steenie's guardians or trustees might do so for her benefit in justice to their ward.

Poor Sutro! It was a bitter notion, and one that made his face grow pale as he contemplated it. He did n't want to die; he loved life dearly — dearly! Even at this strange East, where it rained whenever it felt like it, and not at stated seasons when people were prepared for it and duly expectant — as at San' Felisa, — even here, and with disagreeable Resolved Tubbs " to boot," existence had many pleasures, — not the least among these being Mary Jane's excellent cookery. To die — to put himself forever out of the reach not only of the Little Un, but of Mazan to whom he had hoped to be reunited, and of delicious chicken-patties, all at one fell swoop — that was too much !

"Very well, then. I will delay the evil day, no? They are not suffering now; and if this thousand dollars is not paid yet — why, when it falls due, there will still be time ! *En verdad.* Is it not so, Señor Juez?"

"I do not understand you, Caballero; but if you have finished your directions I will put aside these notes for the present. The will shall be duly drawn up and read to you; when, if satisfactory, it can be attested by your own chosen witnesses. It is about time for me to take my second lesson in colt training; and before I go, I want to ask you if you have heard the Calthorp family speak of this great bank failure, which has ruined so many?"

"Have I not? *Si?* Is it not that which has prompted, this day so soon, the *testamento?* That, but for this sudden poverty, I could have postponed till some far away *mañana* [future]. Señor Tubbs says that my people have become poor —

poor — poor. My Señor Calthorp goes into his
room and broods and broods; and Señora, the
Madam, she smiles, — but with pale lips and
heavy eyes. Ah, it is cruel, cruel! I do not
understand. I am no — what shall I say? Here,
in my head, it is not clear to comprehend this
'business' of the Americans, I. It was that
'business' which was wrong when Santa Felisa
Rancho passed from my family to other men. It
is 'business' again, — a 'bank,' which is worst of
all, — and, lo! to-day our pockets burst with
the gold, to-morrow they hold not a coin. *Por
Dios!* It is all wrong — "

The Judge listened gravely. The flying rumors
he had heard were confirmed by Sutro's statement. He had known, all along, that his old
friends would be losers to some extent by this
failure; but the fact that it involved their all was
new to him and very painful. How to assist
them would be the question. The legal advice he
could give them would be theirs without the asking; but if the reports were wholly true, they
would need something besides legal advice to put
the bread into their mouths.

"Papa! Are you never coming? We were
as good as we could be, yesterday; but we were
better to day! And we were let off from study

five minutes before the eleven o'clock. Come,
please! Won't you? I want to see you and
Diablo take your lesson, now Steenie and I have
done."

Beatrice's interruption was a pleasant relief to
the sombre thoughts of both lawyer and client;
and Diablo's owner answered, promptly, "Oh!
oh! That is all, is it? Revenge? You wish to
see somebody else suffer the torture which the
last two hours have been to you? Eh? For
lessons and torture are synonyms in your book-
hating mind, I fancy, my daughter."

"Now, Papa Courtenay! 'Xcuse me, but it's
no such thing. You're teasing me. And I
should n't think it hard work just to play with
a colt!"

"Should you not? Unless I mistake my val-
iant small girl, entirely, I think it would take a
deal of persuasion to make her exchange even her
dull lessons for mine!"

At which playful irony Beatrice pouted, then
laughed good-naturedly. She had now no ambition horseward, beyond riding a very gentle old
pony at odd times; but she did enjoy the spec-
tacle of others doing that which she feared.

"And how about you, Miss Steenie? Are you
anxious to resume your 'teaching'?"

"Oh, yes, sir! I am a'most hungry to see Diablo! I told Papa 'bout' him; an' he said, 'Then you're happy, dearie!' and I am. Horses are so dear and lovely. They are so — so — what is it when you love anything and it loves you back?" asked Steenie, who had slipped her hand into one of Judge Courtenay's, while his own little daughter held fast to the other.

"Responsive may be the word. But what is Sir Tito being brought along for? Is he to be introduced to Diablo?"

"Ye-es. But that was n't the first, the truly why. I — I have — there's something I want to ask you, by-and-by. That is, do you own that big race-track over yonder, as Sutro says?"

"Yes. I had it prepared for speeding my own horses; but some of the neighbors use it also. I am anxious to increase the interest, hereabouts, in well-bred stock, and so we have trials on it occasionally. By the way, there is to be a public affair soon. The very best horses in the county are entered for the contest, — prizes, and so forth. I am quite anxious and doubtful over the result; for, till now, my black filly Trix has carried everything before her. But Doctor Gerould, of South Knollsboro, has just bought the famous Mordaunt, and I fear my lady Trix will be hard pushed this time."

"Isn't it funny, Steenie? My mama says that Papa would rather win that race than the biggest 'case' that ever was! She says live horses are his hobby-horses, 'at he rides to death! 'Cause she says 'at a'most every rich man finds out some way to use money foolishly, an' Papa's way is the goodest way there is, maybe."

"Come, come, Miss Beatrice! Retailing family affairs for a stranger's benefit?" asked the father, pinching his little girl's cheek, roguishly.

"Steenie an' Sutro aren't strangers, are they? They're just — us, I thought."

"'Just us' — quite right. But here we are! Now, my fine fellow, look out for yourself!"

"I'll go in first with this halter, please. Then you can come when I call you," said the small mistress of ceremonies, and vaulted over the paling, lightly and joyously.

There was no pretence about the sincerity of her pleasure. Her sparkling eyes and dimpling face declared that without words; and, to his utter amazement, Judge Courtenay saw that the pleasure was mutual, for, instead of showing fear or resentment, or any trace of forgetfulness,

up marched Diablo, with all the eagerness in the
world, and extended his handsome nose with a
neigh of salutation.

"Well — well — well! Has the age of mira-
cles returned?" exclaimed the observer, almost
unable to believe his own eyes.

But when Diablo's friendliness was forced to
extend to himself, and when, after an hour or
two of a "lesson" which the gray-haired pupil
enjoyed beyond expression, he was able to lead
the "unbreakable brute" quietly out of the
paddock to the "track," his delight knew no
bounds.

"Upon my word, my little lady, I am your
debtor to a very great extent. I am ready to
give you anything you ask!"

"Huyler's!" suggested Beatrice, in an eager
whisper. "Ask him for 'Huyler's' — do!"

"No conspiracy! What's that you're whis-
pering, missy?"

"Now, Papa! You said 'anything,' and I
thought — candy."

"Is 'Huyler's' candy? Pooh! I don't care
for that. I want you to do something, though,
Beatrice. Will you?"

"Course. What?"

"Let me show you how to ride. On my own

Tito, that nobody ever rode but me, that could be helped, that — Oh, you know ! "

" Why ?   What for ? "

" 'Cause.   Won't you ? "

" Will he run away ? "

" He never did such a mean thing in all his darling life ! Swing her up, dear Sutro, please ! "

Sutro lifted Beatrice, who uttered a little squeal, half of terror, half of pleasure, and placed her squarely on Steenie's own comfortable saddle.   Then followed "lesson two," while the Judge continued his own experiments in horse-training on another part of the course. At the close of which, all came gayly together at the entrance, and not a face showed any care, — not even Sutro's, who had now relegated to that convenient " mañana " of his, the time when he should " die."

" Really, little Steenie, can I not serve you in some practical way ?   I wish to do so most heartily," asked the master of Rookwood, gratefully.

" Yes, sir.   You can give me some advice. I mean if you will," answered she.

" Heigho ! my practice is increasing ! " thought the legal magnate.   Aloud he said : " To the best of my ability."

"I want to earn some money. I want to show other little girls how to ride, same as I showed Beatrice, here. An' maybe to teach other folks horses, too, like Diablo. 'Cause we're 'ruined,' Grandmother says; an' she's an old lady, an' my father's blind, an' — an' — Can I?"

"Wh-e-ew! You baby, you!"

A hurt, indignant flush rose into Steenie's eager face, and her lip trembled.

"There, there! My dear child! It was only astonishment — admiration — which made me say that! Don't misunderstand me. You can do anything — anything — which you set out to do, you — you — brave little thing!"

With that the Judge wheeled sharply round, and tears gathered in somebody's eyes, but not in Steenie's.

CHAPTER XIII.

SUTRO.

MY dear, suppose you let our friend Sutro, here, ride home and tell your people that I am going to keep you for dinner? Then they will not be anxious, and we will have leisure to consider this matter thoroughly. What do you say?" The Judge's tone, addressing Steenie, was as grave an considerate as if she had been Madam Calthorp herself, and it restored her wounded pride at once.

Nobody likes being laughed at, least of all a child, about whose earnestness there is never any pretence. "Baby" had been a hard word for ambitious ears to hear.

"Thank you. I should be as glad as glad to stay! If — my grandmother said I was never to 'trude upon your 'family life;' that just 'cause you asked me to study with Beatrice, I must n't forget an' be too — something or other. It meant I must n't go round an' be a 'noosance,' like Sutro is to Mr. Tubbs."

" 'Noosance'! She could n't be a 'noosance,' could she, Papa Courtenay?" cried Beatrice, dancing gayly about her friend, delighted with the prospect of a visit.

"Never," responded the Judge, cordially. "Señor Vives, it is settled, then. Please convey my regards to Madam Calthorp and her son, and say to them that I will give myself the pleasure of calling upon them toward nightfall, and will bring this little girl with me. Your own affair — the legal document — shall, also, be duly arranged. Good day."

"I have the happiness to salute thee, Señor Juez. In verity, I am proud of the honor done my little one. I will discharge thy message immediately. Ten thousand thanks. *Adios.*" With the lightness of youth the old Spaniard sprung upon Tito's back, doffed his sombrero, bowed profoundly, and rode cheerfully away.

"How funny! It's a side-saddle, too," said Beatrice.

"Yes. But that makes no difference to my

caballero. He can ride in any way on any animal, and always well. My father says he is a wonderful old man; but he does n't seem any older'n me, I think. He 's very good an' dear. My grandmother says 'at Sutro is worth everything to my father now, in his blindness."

"I should think so, indeed! And now for dinner. After that — for a talk about this teaching business. A race to the house! Here we go! And a box of that coveted 'Huyler's' to the winner! Step — step — step! One — two — three! Off!" Away flashed the gay frocks, up and down flew the little black-stockinged legs, and long before the Judge had covered half the distance, the children sat cuddled together on the piazza-step, hugging each other in the exuberance of their love and happiness. "It 's so puffectly nice to have a little girl, same 's me!" cried Steenie, ecstatically. "I used to have the 'boys' an' nobody else. I did n't know 'bout girls, then, an' the 'boys' are dear as dear! But I like girls, now I 've seen 'em, — some girls."

"Me? Do you like me?"

"Course I do. Was n't I just telling you? Say, would you like to ride in a circus?"

"My — sake! No! Would you?"

"Course. I have, — lots of times."

"Why — Steenie — Calthorp! Where? When?
How? Who let you?"

"Out home. Santa Felisa. Ever so many
whens. Last one, just before we came away;
to show the Plunketty man — Lord — what his
own ranchmen could do. My father let me.
Course."

"Was he nice?"

"Who?"

"The Plunketty man-lord. What is a man-
lord, any way?"

"Think I did n't say it right. I mean lord-
man. That is an Englishman. My father says
he can't find land enough in their little bit o'
island to buy, so he came to California an' bought
San' Felisa. But he did n't come again for
twelve years, a'most. An' I never saw him, an'
then I did; an' he did n't wear a cor'net at all!
And he laughed like anything when I told him
what Suzan said. An' he 'xplained beautiful.
He does have the cor'net, but he does n't have it
for himself. It 's his houses'. An' sometimes
the women of 'his house' wear it, when they
'want to make a stunnin' show of theirselfs.'
But mostly they 'have more sense,' an' leave it

where it b'longs, 'mongst the family plates an'
' gew-gaws.'   That 's what he told me."

" Gew-gaws?   Ginger!   Was he a really,
truly, lively lord?   Was he?"

" Live as anything.   Live as you.   Live as me
or your papa.   But, Beatrice, you should n't say
' ginger.'   My grandmother says it 's not c'rect
to use 'spressions."

" But there *is* — ginger!   The cook puts it in
molasses-cake.   So there!"

" Well.   It 's c'rect enough to eat, I s'pose.
But little gentlewomen should show they 's little
gentlewomen by their languages.   So my grandmother says, an' she knows.   'Cause she knows
everything in this whole world."

" She could n't!   She is n't big enough.   My
papa says nobody knows everything.   An' he
talks mostest 'bout grammar, not gentlewomens.
He would n't let you say ' hisself ' or ' theirselfs,' —
I mean if he could help it.   'Cause he would n't
me.   An' I know better 'n you, you see, 'cause
I 've been teached longer."

" Well, I s'pose you do.   Though my grandmother 's c'rected me lots o' times 'bout them
very same words.   I — Only I forget.   My
forgettery is always easier 'n my memory.   Is n't
yours?   An' anyhow I don't know anything,

'cept 'bout horses. But I know more 'bout them 'an I could tell you 'in a month o' Sundays.'"

"How long is a 'month o' Sundays?' When does it come? Before Christmas?"

"I don't know. Mary Jane knows. She talks 'bout it. An' it comes — why it must come any time! 'Cause when Mr. Resolved goes to market she tells him not to be a 'month o' Sundays,' or she can't get the dinner cooked in time. And — lots — Here's your papa! Oh, I tell you I love him! He's so dear."

"You need n't! He is n't yours. You can't have him," cried Beatrice, feeling her young heart swell with jealousy.

"But I can love him, can't I? If you could n't love my father you would be funny. And, oh, is n't it happy to be so glad! Most always, anyhow, I think this is an awful nice world. Folks are so cosey an' kind."

"An' I don't think it's nice one bit. You'll get the candy; I know you will. You got here first!"

"Well — if I did? Would n't I give you half, — the evenest half we could measure? S'pose I'd want it if you did n't have it too? Say, s'pose they'll be dinner enough?"

"What do you mean? Course they will."

"Then I'm glad.   But you see they did n't
know I was coming; an' Mary Jane says I'm
the 'beatenest eater for a little girl she ever
saw;' an' sometimes when comp'ny comes to
my grandmother's she scolds, Mary Jane does.
'Cause she says: 'I have enough cooked for my
own folks, but not enough for my neighbors,' an'
it makes her angry.   An' my grandmother says,
solemn-like: 'Ma-ry-Ja-ne!' an' then Mary Jane
goes in the kitchen an' bangs things around; an'
Mr. Tubbs laughs, an' she gets madder, an' — I
should n't like to make your cook feel that
way."

"Don't you be afraid!   You can have all you
want to eat; an' if they is n't enough you can
have mine, too.   I ain't ever hungry."

"My!   Thank you.   You 're a lovely, nice
girl.   But I would n't eat it.   Why are n't you
hungry?   There 's the bell!"

Away they ran dinner-wards, and found the
Judge rehearsing to his wife the incidents of the
morning, and evidently something of Steenie's
ambition; for the lady bestowed upon the child
a caress more cordial even than usual, and called
her a "dear, brave, helpful little thing."

There proved to be not only enough of food
but to spare; and when the meal was over Judge

Courtenay retired to his office with his secretary, while the children went into the parlor, where Steenie was asked to tell her hostess all about her desired "riding-school," and what had suggested it to her.

"It was the blacksmith made me think about it, when he shod Tito. He said I 'ought to;' an' I s'pose maybe he knows 'bout my father being blind, an' my grandmother an old lady that never did anything but read books, an' they both being so 'helpless,' Mr. Tubbs says. But he, Mr. Resolved, thought I was 'helpless,' too; only I don't want to be. 'Cause I'm not old nor blind, an' I'm strong as anything. But I don't know very much, 'cept 'bout horses; an' I do know 'bout them, way through. So — well, you see — after the blacksmith talk — I thought an' thought — an' thought. First off, it made me dizzy — just the thinking. Then I wasn't dizzy any mor͟ for being sorry — but just for glad! An' I hurried home fast as fast; an' there was my father taking a nap, 'cause he doesn't sleep good nights; an' after supper some comp'ny came, an' they stayed till I went away to bed. Then this morning there they were again; an' they were a man an' his clerk, or something, an' my grandmother an' my father went into the library an' shut the door, so I did n't have any chance to ask him. Then when I was coming here, I thought maybe I was glad I had n't. 'Cause my grandmother says your Mr. Judge is a terr'ble wise gentleman; an' I know so too. An' I thought prob'ly he knew all the little girls an' colts in Old ·Knollsboro; an' maybe they 'd like to learn to ride the right way. And the blacksmith said I 'd 'make a fortune' showing 'em. I 'd like to make it, or some money, I mean. Any way if I could do one thing to buy beefsteaks with, I ought to, had n't I? 'Cause Mr. Tubbs says, 'The Lord only knows how long any on us 'll eat beefsteak,' — an' we all like it. Even my grandmother does. It would be awful, would n't it, for an old lady like her to not have any more?"

"Yes, my dear, it would be very bad indeed; but I hope matters are not quite so serious as that," answered Mrs. Courtenay, smilin.

"Well, I don't know, course. But Mary Jane says we 'd all 'better be lookin' out to earn an honest penny, those on us 'at can.' An' Mr., her brother, said she 'need n't cast no 'flections on him, 'cause had n't he got the lumbago, he 'd like to know?' So, you see, it 's just this one straight way: Grandmother can't, 'cause she

can't, an' she ought n't to ; Papa can't, 'cause he
can't see to do anything ; Sutro can't, 'cause he 's
just Sutro ; Mr. Tubbs can't, 'cause he's a lum-
bagorer an' a ' reg'lar funeral-dark-sider,' Mary
Jane says ; Mary Jane can't, 'cause her ' hands
an' heart is full every 'durin' minute, an' so she
tells you ; ' an' so, after them, they is n't anybody
left but me. So I want to ; 'cause I love 'em
— love 'em — love 'em — every one ! An' I 'm
young, an' I can see, an' I have n't any lumbago,
an' I 'm not just Sutro, an' my hands an' heart
is n't full, and — do — you s'pose I can ? ''

" My dear little girl, I have perfect faith that
you can ! — providing that your people will consent," answered Mrs. Courtenay, with the most
confident of smiles, and very shining eyes.

" Why should n't they consent ? Would n't
they be the most gladdest they could be ? 'Cause
I 'd give them the money, an' they could buy the
things."

" Who told you about ' money,' and money-
earning, Steenie ? '' asked the lady, somewhat
curiously, wondering how a child brought up " in
the wilderness " had learned its value.

" Why, Sutro. I asked him what it meant to
be ' ruined,' an' he told me. He 's ruined, himself, he says ; anyhow he 's lost his home, same

as Grandmother 'll have to lose hers; an' he says
that he had to go to work an' earn money, an'
that was why he did n't 'starve to death, *en
verdad!*' I should think it would be dreadful
to starve to death, should n't you?"

"I certainly should."

"You see Sutro — I don't know 'xactly how it
was. But when I was as little as little, my father
told Sutro 'at if he 'd tend to me an' not let anything bad ever happen to me, he 'd pay Sutro
money. Wages, it 's called. So they did it; an'
Sutro was my body-servant forever after that.
Papa paid him every month, 'cause it was n't the
Plunkett man's money at all.. An' Sutro has
saved it. An' I don't know. He showed me
most of it 'at he had n't spended; an' it does
seem funny that folks 'll give you food an'
clothes an' things just for it; but he says yes.
An' if I earn, an' he helps me, don't you see?
Oh, I hope they will let me, don't you?"

"I — hardly know. I wish you to be happy
with all my heart; and so I mean that you shall
succeed — if they are willing. But they are a
proud family, — the very leading family of Old
Knollsboro; and they may feel it — well. not
just the thing for the little daughter of the
house to teach even a 'riding-school.' But

we'll see. By the way, where would you like to hold your school? Tell me all that you have thought about it, please."

"Why, on your race-course. Why not?" asked Steenie, brightly and innocently.

"Why, Steenie Calthorp! My papa's race-track is my papa's! He won't let anybody, 'cept them he invites, go on it, not once at all. He says it's private, for his own 'musement, an' if folks want tracks let 'em have their own. He wouldn't let other little girls, 'cept you an' me, ride their ponies there, ever; would he, Mama?"

"I cannot answer for another, even your father, my dear. But I think that some fitting place could be found," replied the mother, quietly.

Steenie looked up quickly. Her big blue eyes were filled with astonishment, and a pink flush stole deeper and deeper into her pretty face. Her native instinct, the instinct of a gentlewoman, told her that she had blundered in some way, yet she could not see how. If Judge Courtenay was her friend, — why, he was! — and that was the end of it. Why should he draw the line anywhere?

"Please, Mrs. Courtenay, was I 'truding then? Grandmother said I was never to do that. She said I had lived in a beau-tiful big, big place like

Santa Felisa, an' I was used to being mistress of
everything; but I was to 'member that here, in
this little bit o' Old Knollsboro, I was only a
little bit o' girl. But if the dear Judge does n't
want me to use his course, why I can find a
place, somewhere, big enough. I guess maybe
the blacksmith can tell me. He was a very
nice man, too."

Mrs. Courtenay watched the troubled little face
grow bright and sunny again, and then she sent
the children out to play; after which an elegant
carriage was brought round, and a groom in livery
assisted the lady into it, and lifted Beatrice to a
place beside her. But Steenie needed no assistance, and was quite contented when the Judge
took the empty seat next her, and she heard
the order given, "To Madam Calthorp's, High
Street."

It was a gay and happy party, and they carried
their own good cheer with them into the care-
shadowed home which they entered, — the greet-
ings of the elders being even more cordial and
sympathetic than ever, could that have seemed
possible.

Nothing, not even heart-break, could make
Madam Calthorp other than the noble, gracious
woman she had always been; and no sign of the

14

burden she was bearing was permitted to inflict itself upon her guests. Yet even her self-reliant spirit gained fresh courage from the support of these friends whom she held in such high esteem; and she was delicately forced to remember that the Judge would be honored if she would make use of him in any way.

"Yes, Steenie, show Beatrice anything. And you will find some roses in the garden, the sort her mother likes. Thank you; but, Judge, such things are usually very simple. I have had one of the bank men here over night. There is nothing left, absolutely, beyond my trifling amount of real estate. I shall put this house on the market, and dispose of it as speedily as possible. I have already written to accept an offer which I had for the little farm; and — that is all. If you hear of a small cottage anywhere in town, that is not in an objectionable neighborhood, will you kindly let me know? And now — let us talk about your horses. I'm sure that Daniel will enjoy a description of them. He is quite a horse-lover, though not like Steenie — all horse! Did you ever know a taste so marked? It amounts almost to a passion with her; due to her training at Santa Felisa, I suppose. Well, it has made her a perfectly healthy

and wonderfully happy child. I am grateful to
the odd rearing for that much, at least."

"And for much more! — that is, you may be!"
returned the Judge, impulsively. His heart was
still glowing warmly with thoughts of Steenie's
brave desire, and the words escaped him almost
unconsciously.

"Indeed! How so? I fear that even her
last intercourse with the equine race is about
over for poor little Steenie."

"It should not be. No, no; it must not be!
— that would be a crime. Let me tell you,
please," and the gentleman described, far more
minutely and eloquently than the little girl had
done, her marvellous influence over Diablo, and
her instruction of himself. He concluded en-
thusiastically: "It is her gift — Heaven-sent!
She is the best friend the horse ever had, I
believe. And that child's beneficent influence
is destined to work a complete revolution, hereabouts, in the future treatment of the noble
animals. It is as if she had a magical power of
entering into their very feelings, inclinations,
joys, and sufferings. I never witnessed anything
like it! Yet the only explanation she can give
is: 'It is n't anything I do. I don't know how
to explain it — only I just love them so!' My

dear Madam, your grandchild is a phenomenon. Better than that — she is the bravest, noblest little creature who ever lived."

"Judge, Judge! You are too enthusiastic, and too kind!" answered Steenie's amazed grandmother.

"Enthusiastic, perhaps; but I could not be too kind to a child like that. It is an honor to serve her. She has taught me, not only what a fool I have been about horses, but how to meet trouble, disaster. Listen to this: here is her idea — that baby's!"

Launched upon his subject, Judge Courtenay poured out the whole story. Steenie's half-formed plans had taken full shape and detail under the consideration of his own maturer mind, and not only this, but he had actually decided, mentally, upon the children to be selected for her first pupils. He could not see one good reason why the project was not wholly feasible, with Sutro and himself to "back" it with age and experience.

"She shall have the course at Rookwood for ordinary weather; and I will have a great building erected for stormy days. I know several persons who have valuable colts, and they will gladly avail themselves of her gentle method of 'breaking in.' They shall pay her well, too! The school terms we will regulate by those of city riding-schools; and she shall have the use of as many of my horses as is necessary, besides her own Tito. That old Sutro is just the fellow to assist; and my grooms shall do the rough work."

"Pardon me, Judge, but it appears to me as if this were to be your school, — not my little daughter's!" exclaimed Mr. Calthorp, smilingly.

"All right — all right! Make it so, then! Let it be my institution, and she my salaried instructor. Why not? That is an improvement upon the original plan, — decidedly an improvement. People will be less inclined to shirk their tuition fees to me, a grim old lawyer, maybe, than to her. Yet I think she would never lose a penny. How could she, — if men and women are human?"

Mrs. Courtenay had been observing their hostess, and interrupted, gently : "My dear, you are taking for granted the consent of Steenie's guardians. However, I trust it will not be wanting." The speaker noticed, regretfully, that the children had returned, and that the little subject of the discussion was standing on the threshold of the room, her lithe young body eagerly poised and her eyes intently watching her grandmother's face for the answer forthcoming, which was made speedily and courteously, but it struck upon Steenie's heart with intolerable cruelty.

"Thank you, cordially, my dear friend. Your generous kindness is fully appreciated — fully. But I have already reached a more practical decision, — one which will put more money, even, into Steenie's pocket than this chimerical, if unselfish scheme of hers could ever do. We will sell Tito. Do you know of a purchaser?"

In the silence which followed this unexpected suggestion, Steenie heard her own heart beat. Then she bounded into the centre of the room, white with fear and indignation.

"Grandmother! Sell — my — Tito!"

"Yes, darling. We can no longer afford to keep him."

"You must n't! You must n't! It would break his very heart! I 'd rather you 'd sell me!"

CHAPTER XIV

FOR a time nobody said anything more. Then Madam Calthorp resumed, but in a very kindly and sympathetic tone: "Yes, my darling, we can no longer indulge in any luxury."

Steenie found courage to speak again. "I don't know what that is. But Tito isn't a 'luxury,' is he? He's just a dear, darling little horse!"

"POOR MR. TUBBS."

"Which, under our changed circumstances, means that he is a luxury, as well."

"You mustn't! You shall not! You dare not! He's mine — mine — mine!"

"Steenie!" said the father, in a pained voice, and opening his lips for the first time.

The child flew to him in a passion of tears. "She can't — she — she — He's folks! He can't be sold. It would — break — his very — heart!"

Touched by the distress of her little friend, Beatrice grew angry and resentful also, and darted to her own father, who put his arm about her and kissed her, glad of anything upon which to vent his emotion; for it must be owned that the big, wise man was almost as vexed and uncomfortable as the two children were.

Mrs. Courtenay walked over to the bay-window and examined an album of etchings, trying, but failing, to appear at ease. To all present it was a very unpleasant scene.

Yet there was no disputing the plain common-sense of Madam Calthorp's decision, who, it is also true, had no real conception of the strength of the bond between the child and her beloved four-footed friend, her only playmate during all her little life.

Steenie had parted from Tito at Santa Felisa, bravely and cheerfully as she could, "for Papa's sake;" but she had believed it to be a parting for a time, merely. She had then full faith in the cure of her father's blindness, which was to be effected by some unknown physician in an equally unknown "East;" and she had looked forward to a joyful return and reunion, when everything and everybody was to be even happier than before.

Now she knew better what " trouble " meant; and to part with Tito forever seemed like cutting her own heart in two.

" Steenie, my granddaughter! Do not forget that there are others present to whom an exhibition of domestic misunderstanding must be most disagreeable. You may take the basket of sea-shells into the dining-room, if you like, and show them to Beatrice."

" I don't care about sea-shells, ma'am," responded Beatrice, with what she considered great politeness.

" An' — an' — please 'xcuse me! " said Steenie, tremulously, and ran out of the house, stable-ward, faster than even her fleet feet had ever sped before.

Mrs. Courtenay rose, " I think, Judge, that it is really time we should go. I have another call to make, and it is growing late. I hope, dear madam, that you are satisfied with Steenie's progress under Miss Allen. She tells me that the little thing is very bright at her studies."

" Thank you; fully satisfied. Yes, I think, I am sure that our little girl has intelligence; only

her instruction has heretofore been so deficient, —
in every way. I trust you will pardon her rudeness, and expect better things of her by-and-by.
She has been a trifle spoiled, I fear. However, I believe that she will make rapid ad-
vancement after she is once well started. And
pray do not think, Judge, that because I found
your 'riding-school' too big a venture for a
child not yet eleven to undertake, that I do
not estimate your own unselfish motive most
highly. It simply — could not be." Madam
Calthorp's smile as she said this was very bright
and very proud.

"That's it! It's the miserable Calthorp pride
that is at the bottom of it!" muttered the Judge,
as he rode away. "The father had more sense;
he saw no objection to our idea any more than I
do, or any other sensible person could. It is
an original scheme, of course; but where would
the world be if it were not for original people
now and then? The child has a talent — a genius
— in a unique line. Well, then, why not develop
it, — same as music, art, or any other great gift?
And she'd be perfectly safe, — I'd see to that;
they must have known it."

"Doubtless they did; and I know something
else."

"What's that?" —a trifle shortly. It does not improve the temper of most people to have their generosity declined, and the Judge was no exception to the rule.

"That you will buy Tito, if he must be sold, and keep him at Rookwood for his own little mistress."

"Or for me, Mama, maybe."

"No, dear Beatrice, for Steenie. Surely you do not wish to take her beloved horse away from her?"

"No, course I don't; but, you see, I thought maybe that old Madam lady would say she could n't have him. 'Cause she 'peared to me 's if she liked to be kind of mis'able an' give up things. Same 's I don't."

"Beatrice!"

"The child is right. Madam Calthorp is a fine woman, but she is as proud as Lucifer. He had to tumble, and she will, or I'm mightily mistaken. It takes a very noble nature to accept favors graciously; and she had an idea that I was conferring, or trying to confer, a favor, which I was not at all. I think it would be the best thing ever happened in this locality, and to the dumb beasts in it, if that blessed, loving little thing could have a chance to preach to us in her innocent way. I mean she shall yet, too! And I suppose that to have a little girl earn anything towards the family support was a bitter motion, also."

"The most bitter, I think, husband. However, we can do nothing more. But we must have Steenie at Rookwood as much as possible. If one is bound to be kind and helpful one can generally find a way, though not always the way first chosen. Remember that, Beatrice, and be watchful for Steenie's happiness."

"Yes, Mama, I think somebody ought to watch it; 'cause herself's bein' comf'table is the last thing she cares about."

"That's right, my darling," said the mother, fondly, as she alighted to pay her second call, and thinking very tenderly of the other little girl who had never known the sweetness of a mother's commendation.

Meanwhile, at the house in High Street, a few earnest words had been said by blind Daniel Calthorp, which touched, if they did not convince, the proud heart of its mistress.

"The scheme is not as wild as it seems, dear mother. If you could see my darling among her friends, the horses, you would understand."

"But to have it said that a child — a little

girl-child — is our maintenance ! Daniel, is it not
absurd ?   Besides, could she actually earn enough
to amount to anything ? "

"I think so.   However, we will not discuss
further to-night, — perhaps not at all.   Only, if
you think it would be difficult for you to accept aid from the hand of a child, what do you
think it is for me — a man ?   My blindness was
not of my own choosing ; and Steenie's talent has
not been given to her for nothing.   Do you remember what my father used to say ? 'God never
shuts one door but He opens another.'   The doors
seem to be pretty fast closed on every side our
lives, just now, Mother.   Was this — one of His
opening ?   Let us find out that ; and — I 'll go
to Steenie now."

"You need not.   She comes here to you,"
and, despite her decision, which had made her
seem so "hard" and stern to her little granddaughter, it was a very proud and loving glance
which rested upon the now dejected face of the
household darling.   "Come here, my little one.
I have something to say to you."

Steenie obeyed ; but she did not raise her eyes
from the floor, and her small hands were clinched
tight together, — in a habit she had adopted to
help "keep the tears back."   She expected a repre-

mand for her rudeness, and she anticipated it. " I
came back — 'cause — my father says — no matter — I must n't never — be anything but nice —
as nice — to you. I did n't mean you — Grandmother; not you — yourself. I — I only —
Tito — "

" Kiss me, Steenie. I understand you fully.
I have quite forgiven anything that there is to
forgive. I should have broken the sad news to
you more gently if I could, but you happened
to overhear it. What I want to tell you, now,
dear, is that I think you are the bravest, dearest
child I ever knew. It was a very kind desire of
yours to help us in the only way which was natural to your peculiar life and training; but what
would do in the far West would hardly answer
here in Old Knollsboro. However, you still have
an opportunity to be brave and kind. I have decided — I trust that your father agrees with me
— that the first sacrifice demanded of you is —
Tito. It is painful to me to ask it; but it is
right. I hope you will meet this trial in the
same spirit which you displayed in this other im-
practicable scheme. May I depend upon you, my
darling ? "

A sob that shook her whole sturdy little body
welled up and broke from Steenie's lips; and

though the great tears now rolled over the round cheeks her blue eyes were raised steadfastly and her dainty mouth forced itself into a smile, so brave and determined, yet so pitiful, that it pierced Madam Calthorp's heart like a knife.

With an impulse foreign to her self-controlled nature she caught her grandchild to her heart, and bent her white head upon the brown curls, while a sympathetic sob escaped her own lips. This was the first actual taste of the poverty which had befallen her household, and she found it bitter indeed.

But from that moment, strange as it seemed to Steenie's own self, she loved her grandmother as she had not done before, and felt so sorry for her that personal grief was almost forgotten.

" Now," said Madam, lifting her head, — " now, what is to be done, I want done quickly; to me waiting and suspense are intolerable. We know that we must leave this house; let us leave it as soon as possible. To-morrow I will advertise it for sale, and hope for a speedy purchaser. Fortunately, High-Street property is rarely offered, and there is always a greater demand than supply. Hark! Is that the supper-bell?"

" Yes, 'm. Come, Papa, dear, I'm hungry, anyhow. And I gave Tito heaps and heaps. But I

think you 'll have to speak to Sutro. He did n't
— he did n't behave very nice. But he — felt
— pretty mis'able, an' — Why, Mr. Tubbs!"

Mr. Tubbs, indeed! Never within Madam Calthorp's memory had that worthy "professor"
entered her presence in such a condition as this.
His hair looked as if it had never been combed;
his spectacles were broken and dangling from his
neck, instead of reposing respectably upon his
bald forehead; his coat was torn and covered
with bits of hay; and — must the truth be
owned? — one pale gray eye was bruised and
half-hidden by the rapidly swelling flesh which
surrounded it; worst indignity of all, he was
being marched into the dining-room by Mary
Jane's forcible grip upon his shoulder, and it was
her disgusted voice which called attention to his
damaged condition.

"Yis! I should say so! 'Mis-ter Tubbs!'
Here he is! A wolf in sheep's clothin'! Him a
Methodist an' a class-leader! Look at him!
Drink him in! He ain't nobody but my brother
— oh, oh, oh!"

"Resolved! Mary Jane! Explain this matter
at once. What has happened?"

"Happened, ma'am? Nothin' but a — fight!
A reg'lar, school-bubby actin' up! It's them two

old simpletons, Sutro an' Resolved. They 've always wrangled an' jangled ever sence they fust sot eyes on one another. But I 've managed ter keep 'em from fisticuffin' up till now. An' him my only brother! A shinin' light in the church, he is! Wait till I get my dishes washed, an' I 'll step down ter Presidin' Elder Boutwell's, an' let him hear what kind o' sperritooal goin's on we have down this way!"

"But why should you and Sutro Vives quarrel, Resolved? What provocation did he give you?" asked Mr. Calthorp, anxiously.

"Nothin' in the world! It 's my poor, sinful old brother here, that 's done all the prov-ockin'! A tellin' that poor heathen old Catholic that they was n't no use fer him here, no more. An' no bread ter fill the mouths o' our own household, let alone Mexicers. When he knowed well enough 't I 'd jest done my reg'lar bakin,' an' no beautifuller never come out o' that oven this hull summer, let alone more. An' then pilin' it on top o' that, how if it had n't a be'n fer him — Sutry — 'at Steenie need n't 'a' gin up her pony! Don't wonder old feller was mad; an' fust he knowed Resolved got a snap-word back — an' then! Well, you know, ma'am, better 'n I kin tell ye, how quer'ls grows. Bad

15

tempers — sass-hatefulness — candles hid — no light shinin' — an' then — blows! Yis, ma'am, — blows!"

"Mary Jane! Those two old men!"

"Nobody elset. I don't wonder ye're dumberfoun', I was myself. But fust whack I heered out I hurried an' there they was! Reg'lar rough an' tumble, right in the hay-mow, afore Teety pony's own eyes; an' I declar', if that knowin' critter did n't actilly 'pear ter be laughin'. An' 'shamed I am ter have lived ter this day! But — so much fer the Methodist doctrine! No, ma'am, nobody need n't tell me 'at anything short o' full 'mersion 'll ever wash the wickedness out o' poor humans like Resolved Tubbs! No, ma'am, ye need n't."

As Madam Calthorp had never "told" anything of the sort, she could afford to smile; and lamentable as the silly affair was, it yet, as a previous "quer'l" had done, served to divert the thoughts of the family from more serious troubles.

"Poor Mr. Tubbs! Naughty Mr. Tubbs! You — look — so funny!" cried Steenie, laughing. "Did my bad, darling old Sutro-boy hurt your lumbago?" And carried away by a mental picture of the strange conflict, she danced about the victim of his own valor in a manner which provoked his smiles, even if it did his anger, also.

"Well — well — hesh up, can't ye? I know — I know as well as anybody 't I'd oughter be ashamed; but — I — but — I — I got that riled I clean fergot everything. Hm-m. The furrin' vagabones! A tellin' — ME — 't 1'd oughter go ter work an' do sunthin' ter help the fambly! 'S if I was n't a doin' all a mortal man could, now! An' a sayin' 't he'd show me! He'd let ever'body know 'at where he gin his heart's love thar he gin his mis'able airthly possessions, as well. He'd show! That tantalizin' like, I felt I'd like ter 'nihilate him. I could n't help it. An' if I did take my poor mites o' savin's — how fur would it go towards keepin' a hull fambly, an' heathen furriners an' circus horses, ter boot, — I'd like ter know?"

"No matter, Tubbs. I am profoundly sorry that you should have quarrelled with anybody on our account, least of all with a poor, dependent old man like the caballero. I agree with Mary Jane, that one who has enjoyed the privileges which you have, here in the East, should have been too wise for any such trumpery nonsense; and I trust that you will duly apologize to Sutro

Vives, and make him forget, if it is possible, your unkind words about his being a burden upon us. Your zeal on our behalf is appreciated; but please consult me before you give expression to it in the future. Enough of this. Serve supper, please, Mary Jane."

Mr. Tubbs escaped to his own apartment, a very astonished and self-disgusted old man. If anybody had prophesied to him such an utter collapse of Christian conduct, he would have scouted the suggestion with scorn. But here was the stubborn fact: he, Resolved Tubbs, a "perfessor an' a beakin light, have gone and buried my candle under the bushel! Jest fer what?"

Mary Jane could have told him in one word what it took him many hours of Bible-reading and self-examination to find out. "Jealousy," Mr. Tubbs, jealousy, the meanest, most obdurate sin that ever gets into a human soul, old or young. to twist it out of shape.

"Well — I'm glad of that! 'Cause I'm hungry. I always am, and I did n't know, first off, whether I'd ought to stay at Mrs. Courtenay's; but they said 'yes,' an' I had a lovely time. Papa, are n't rooks funny? They're English, imported, the Judge says, and they're dozens an' bushels an' more, in those splendid great trees

in the park. That's what makes 'em call it
Rookwood. An' now, soon's I've finished, I'm
goin' to find my poor blessed Sutro Vives. He's
been naughty, course, same's Mr. Resolved has.
Just like they were little boys, is n't it? But he
must n't stay naughty. I could n't 'low that,
could I, Papa? 'Cause he's very, very good
'most always, an' I hope Mary Jane will give
him a nice supper. Can she, Grandmother?
'Cause it must be terr'ble to be told not to eat.
I think — I think — I could do 'most anything
else better than not eat."

"I think you could, sweetheart! But hunger
at your age is both natural and desirable. You
are growing very fast. I can feel that even if I
cannot see it," responded Mr. Calthorp, caressing
the curly head which rested for a moment against
his shoulder.

"And when I find Sutro, I'll make him 'polo-
gize to you, Grandmother; 'cause he ought n't
to fight at your house, anyhow, no matter if he
does sometimes at San' Felisa. I s'pose he's
over his anger by this time, don't you? I can't
bear to see folks angry; it makes me shivery all
inside, and if he is n't I'd rather wait."

"I think you are safe, my dear; and go at once.
I would not have the poor old fellow feel himself

an intruder, now, if I could help it. I fear the plain-spoken Tubbs was not very careful of his remarks."

Steenie departed ; and it was quite lamp-lighting time before she returned, with a very troubled face. "I cannot find my Sutro anywhere. I've looked an' looked, an' called — called — called — low an' loud — but he isn't anywhere at all. And his blanket that he keeps in the hay to take his siesta on is gone, too. What do you s'pose, Papa ?"

"That he probably has gone somewhere to walk off his anger and mortification ; and that he will soon be back."

"It would be awful mis'able if he didn't come back at all, wouldn't it ?"

"Yes ; too miserable to contemplate for a moment. Come, my darling, and sing to me for a little while ; then, most likely, he will return."

But, at that very moment, a solitary old man, in curious attire, and with a gay Navajo blanket folded over his shoulder, was making his way through the gathering twilight toward Rookwood. His head was bowed, and his face hidden by his wide sombrero, and he moved slowly as one whose footsteps are hindered by a heavy heart.

A pathetic figure which the growing gloom receives and hides, the humblest, and the noblest, perhaps, of all those whose hearts have been touched by the love of the child Steenie, he passes thus out of the story of her life at Old Knollsboro.

CHAPTER XV.

MR. TUBBS AND STEENIE.

M R. TUBBS sat with his spectacles in place, his Bible on his knee; and Steenie, peering in at the kitchen-door and seeing it otherwise deserted, would speedily have retreated, had she been allowed. But an outrageous groan from Resolved arrested her flight, and awoke her ready sympathy.

"Is it so bad, poor dear? Is it worser 'n usual?"

"Oh! Ah-h-h!" That sigh appeared to have arisen in the sigher's very feet, it was so long drawn out and so unutterably doleful. "To think I'd a lived ter see this day! Man an' boy, forty odd years, have I been uset ter settin' beside this very fire an' a peroosin' o' Scripters by this very

winder; an' now — My-soul-I-declare, — life
ain't wuth livin'!"

"Oh, pooh! You only feel hypoey, Mary
Jane says. Try an' not think 'bout troubles so
much, please. An' I do think, like she does, 'at
it's the queerest thing your hypoey comes
whenever they's such a lot to do, is n't it? I
know you can't help it, an' it must make you
feel dreadful bad not to be able to help more;
but do try an' not mind it, there's a dear!"

"I'll try; but I ain't the man I uset ter was.
I've got the neuraligy in my head, an' the dys-
repsy in my stummick, an' the lumbago in my back,
an' I ain't a good deal well. You know it, don't ye,
Steenie? Ye're sorry fer the old man, ain't ye?"

"Why, ye-es. But I'm lots sorrier for all the
rest of the folks. My father says it's a'most
more than Grandmother can bear, this leaving
her old home; but *she* does n't go 'Oh!' and
'Ah-h!' over it. She just shuts her lips tight,
an' goes hard to work; an' I guess that's what
you'd better do, dear Mr. Tubbs. It seems to
help he   n' maybe it will you. Why, she's
packed every one o' her 'precious books,' all her
own self, without nobody touching to help her;
an' Mary Jane says it's the best thing she could
have done."

"Some folks hain't no fine feelin's, Steenie. Mary Jane hain't, — I grieve ter say it."

"What makes you, then?'

"Because — be-cause, I tell ye! Here they ain't nobody payin' no 'tention ter me; ner thinkin' o' my — 'motions, a tearin' myself up by the ruts, this 'ere way; an' jest a goin' on as if this break-up wasn't nothin'."

"Well. 'Xcuse me, but I don't see as it is to — you. 'Cause it wasn't your house, see? An' the little new one is cuter than cute! It's as cunning as a doll-house. An' Mary Jane says, 'Make the best on 't, honey, an' thank the Lord it 's in a decent neighborhood!' An' I'm going to do it. Mary Jane Tubbs is a real Christian, my father says."

"Yer 'father says' — 'father says' — tacked onter the end o' every verse! Yer father don't know ever'thing!"

"He does, too, Resolved Tubbs! — Mister, I mean. Everybody says 'at he 's the best man in the world! He can't see a single thing, yet he's going to work an' try an' write down, all in the dark, all 'at he knows 'bout managing a great rancho; an' Judge Courtenay says 'at he 'll get it copied out 'fair an' square,' an' then printed; an' the world 'll have to see that it takes 'more 'n blindness to kill a brave man,' — so there! And he does n't groan, either. Since he 's thought 'bout this book business he 's just as jolly as he used to be, an' never lets Grandmother nor me nor anybody see if he feels bad — not once! S'posin' he got the hypo, too! Would n't Grandmother an' Mary Jane an' me have a terr'ble time, then ?"

" Hm-m. I don't see where Mary Jane 's sech a great Christian ! My-soul-I-declare ! I hain't seen her tetch her Bible once sence we begun ter tear up."

" That 's it ! That 's just it ! My father says 'at she has its teachings so deep down inside her 'at she can't forget them, an' does n't need to read 'em so much. He says her keeping the meals regular an' well-cooked, an' the house sunshiny an' clean, an' herself good-tempered through all her hard work, has taught him a beautiful lesson. Think of it ! Just Mary Jane teaching my papa ! Anyhow, I love her, an' I came to bid her good-by. 'Cause I 'm off to Rookwood an' lessons an' fun, now ! Where is she ? Do you know ?"

" No, ner keer ; an' you 're a ungrateful little girl. Thar I sot, all yisterday arternoon, a crackin' butternuts an' pickin' the meats fer ye —

an' ye never! Well, well; it's a hard kind o' world."

"*Puss-ley!* Do shet up, an' git up an' take a holt o' some kind o' job, brother Resolved! You're enough ter make a critter backslide, a lookin' at yer limpsey-lumpsey laziness!"

"Thar! Thar Steenie Calthorp! Ye hear her? That's yer fine Ch—"

"Please don't quarrel, dear folks! Don't! An' it is n't so bad, is it? We'll all be so cosey an' cunning in the little new house. Good-by, Mary Jane. Dear, dear Mary Jane! I love you! You're so lively an' kind, an' fly-about-y! You make everybody feel so good, dear Mary Jane! Good-by."

At the door the child paused; her conscience upbraided her for manifesting the partiality she could not help feeling, and with a sudden dash across the room, she caught Mr. Tubbs's neck in her arms and gave him a hearty kiss. Then she darted out again, and in a moment was speeding down the street toward Rookwood, where she still went every day, but now quite by herself. Tito had for some weeks been domiciled in Judge Courtenay's roomy stables, and his little mistress saw him daily. Almost daily, also, she had a long ride on his back, so that she scarcely missed him from the High-Street home; and thus one trouble which had seemed unendurable in prospect became quite the contrary in reality.

"Because, you see, Mary Jane, they is n't any nice cunning little barn to keep him in at the new cottage, so I 'm glad after all."

"Yis, dearie; an' so you 'll find out, long 's you live. Trouble is a great hand ter stan' a ways off an' make up faces at ye; an' ye feel 's if ye could n't endure it, no way. But jest you pluck up spunk ever' time, an' march straight up ter the old thing, and there, — lo! an' behold! — she 's a grinnin' an' a smilin' as if she 's the best friend you 've got. An' most the times she is. Folks 'at don't have no real trouble ter git along with, don't gen'ally amount ter shucks. Life ain't all catnip; an' it hain't meant ter be. An' ye better, by far, bear the yoke in yer youth 'an in yer old age."

"Like Mr. Resolved? He 's bearing it now, is n't he, in his old age? Is that what you mean?"

"Not by a jug-full! He ain't a bearin' — nothin'; he 's squat right down under it, an' a lettin' it squash all the marrer o' religion out o' his poor old bones. Foolish brother Resolved!

I 've be'n a bolsterin' an' a highsterin' him up all my life, an' I 'spect I 'll have ter continuer on ter the end. No matter; I did n't have the choosin' o' my own trials er I would n't a chose that kind o' relations. An' the good Lord is a lookin' out fer poor Mary Jane; so why should she bother ter look out fer herself ? "

Even the sorrow of losing Sutro had taken on a softer aspect when, after his first night's absence, Steenie learned from Judge Courtenay that the old caballero had been at Rookwood just at nightfall, had remained long enough to " transact some business " with himself, and then had started on a late train across the continent to Santa Felisa. The Judge had also given her Sutro's last loving message : —

" Tell, *mi niña,* that her love has made old Sutro Vives a better man. That he could not stay to be a burden to anybody; that he 'll be well and happy in the spot where he was born ; and that he goes to make his last home on his own property of Santa Trinidad. *Caramba !* He will rest well, with old Californian soil for his bed, and Californian sunshine for his blanket. Thou wilt say to her these words, Señor Juez ? "

When the gentleman answered warmly : "I will do everything I can for your ' Little Lady of the Horse,' Señor Vives; I will carry out your instructions to the letter," Sutro murmured: "Ten thousand thanks, most generous. *Gracias a Dios!* I shall see San' Felis once more!" and departed.

But all this was sometime past; and as Steenie went now to Rookwood, the brilliant autumn leaves were beginning to fade on the paths, and the Michaelmas daisies bloomed thickly by the roadside. She passed along, 'a gay, cheerful, loving little maiden, feeling that the world held but one trouble for her now, and that one so far beyond her power to remove, that she was trying to "march straight up to it," and see if it would smile at her, as Mary Jane had said.

The trouble has probably been foreseen; and Judge Courtenay put it into words for her as she danced up to the porch where he was pacing, and swept him a grave, graceful Spanish "courtesy," that she had learned "at home" from dark-eyed Suzan'.

"Good-morning, good-morning, Miss Sunbeam! You look as bright as if we elder people were not worrying our heads off this 'minute! So when does the 'flitting' occur? The removal from High Street to that miserable cottage?"

"To-morrow, sir, thank you! An', please

'xcuse me, but it is n't mis'able. It's as pretty as it can be, I think."

"And 'I think' settles it, eh? Well, well; you ought to thank Heaven for your temperament! Now if I only had it, I should n't be feeling this minute angry enough to 'bite a tenpenny nail in two.'"

Down sat the funny gentleman in the big Plymouth rocker, and opened his arms to "his other little girl," who nestled in them quite as confidently and almost as lovingly as Beatrice would have done. "Why, sir, whatever can be the matter to make *you* — look cross?"

"I look it, too, do I? — as well as feel it. Hm-m. Thank you. Children, et cetera, — truth, you know. First reason, please: I'm deserted. My wife and daughter are busy with all these guests, and I've had to retreat to the schoolroom for a bit of quiet."

"Never mind. They have to be p'lite, I s'pose. My grandmother says 'at folks who live in high stations, like you do, owes great 'sponsibilities to s'ciety an' its demandings."

"Your grandmother is an oracle! She's making you one. But draw up that other chair and hear me grumble; it does me good to express myself to somebody. My wife says that I cannot

keep anything, save clients' business, to myself.
Hm-m. What do you think of that?"

"I s'pose she knows, prob'ly. But am I to
have no lessons?"

"No. Not unless you are suffering to rattle
off: 'I have been, thou hast been or you have
been, he has been,' — and all the rest of it.
Seems to me I heard you say, yesterday, that
you thought grammar was not very 'exciting,'
eh?"

"Oh! no, sir, it is n't! And if I could have
a holiday, maybe Diablo could have another
waltzing lesson, could n't he? He's such a
graceful, teachable horse, I love him!"

"So do I, thanks to your wise interpretation
of his character. But Diablo is n't in to-day's
programme. And I 'm greatly disturbed, absurdly
disturbed, for such a foolish cause. However, I
cannot help it, cannot throw it off."

"Can I help it? I wish I could! What is
the thing 'at disturbs you?"

"The afternoon's race."

"Why — what? I thought everything was all
fixed. I hope it is n't given up, is it?"

"Not yet. Nor do I like to postpone it;
but — There comes John with a telegram. I
hope a favorable one."

16

The race referred to was a proposed contest for supremacy to be held at the " private track" of Rookwood, between the Courtenay horses and those of neighboring county magnates. As has been said before, that part of the state was famous for its fine stock ; and these millionnaire owners of world-renowned animals spared no expense in the indulgence of their equine " hobby," or the furtherance of their ambition to lead in the matter of speed and purity of breed.

Steenie had been deeply interested in the preparations, and her heart beat in sympathy with a distress she had now learned was connected with the day's event.

" Pshaw! It's too bad! Too contemptibly pitiful and mean ! I can't get the other jockey, either!" exclaimed the Judge, thrusting the yellow missive behind him, and striding up and down the school-room porch.

Steenie waited but a moment, then she stole to his side, slipped her warm little hand into his great palm, and made an absurd attempt with her own shorter limbs to equal the pace of her perplexed friend.

" Hm-m. You good little thing! But even your encouragement can't help me now."

" Would you just as lief tell me what it is?

Maybe I could help, maybe. I'm awful anxious to, 'cause, 'cause — you're so good to me an' every single body. Maybe I can."

"I wish you could! If you were a boy! Hm-m. No use. Yet it is so trying to be balked by a little thing like that!"

"Like what, sir?"

"Oh, you persistent little monkey! There — you know I mean that for a compliment! Come then, sit you down and hear an old simpleton's trouble, then laugh at him as you laugh at all annoyance."

"But not folks. Dear Judge Courtenay, I don't mean to laugh at folks."

"You don't! Listen. You know Lady Trix?"

"Course."

"You know she's fast, don't you?" ·

"Faster 'n lightning!"

"Pretty near, I declare. Well, you know, also, that boy Tretter who was going to ride her against Doctor Gerould's Mordaunt?"

"Yes. Well?"

"Anything but well! That imp has gone and tumbled off a wood-shed roof, playing circus, and broke his leg."

"Oh, my! Poor Tretter!"

"Poor Tretter? Poor Courtenay! Lady Trix

was never ridden by anybody else, at any such time as this. He was just right weight, and had a good head, — or I thought that he had till this performance."

"But I s'pose he could n't help it."

"Could n't help it? What did he get up there for, any way? I 'd have given him a thousand dollars to stay off that roof, — or at least to postpone the leg-break for another twenty-four hours."

Steenie gazed at her old friend's face in astonishment; then her own countenance flushed. "Oh, I said maybe I could help you, and I can — I can!"

"What? Do you know any jockey round here, worth a cent? One that Trix will bear?" asked the other, eagerly.

"No, sir. I ain't 'quainted with any jockeys in Old Knollsboro; but *I* — can ride her."

There was utter silence for an instant, and the horse-fancier's face brightened. "You?" Then it sobered again. "Thank you, dearie, but that would n't answer."

"Why would n't it? I 'm sure I could! And I want you to win; I do, I do! I 'd be so glad! Do let me try?"

"Steenie Calthorp, don't tempt me; in a case like this my will is water!"

"But why not?   Don't you know that I could?
Have n't you seen me ride Diablo bareback, —
standing — sitting — every way?   And once, before I knew how 'ticular you were 'bout her, I
came dreadful near riding Trixie myself, — I did,
indeed, only Beatrice told me better.   But I could.
May n't I?"

"I want to win!"

"I will."

"How do you know?"

"Try me; please try me! You 've done things
an' things an' things — for me; an' now — please
let me do this wee, wee little thing for you."

"Wee?   It 's a tremendous undertaking."

"Pouf!"   Steenie shrugged her shoulders in
one of her little Spanish fashions, and made a
motion of blowing thistle-down from her finger-
tips.   "Wait till I tell you. Do sit down a
minute, please.   I can ride anything.   I can
ride standing, an' jumping through rings, an'
over hurdles, an' any way a horse can go I can
ride.   If you 'll let me show you now, — once
this morning, — before everybody much is on the
track, I 'll make you see.   Then you 'll say yes,
won't you?"

"Steenie — I 'm — I 'm wax. But your grandmother —   Do with me as you will!" cried the

Judge, comically, but looking very much relieved. " And there certainly is no harm in your riding Trixie once, now — as you say."

Within the next half-hour Steenie demonstrated fully her ability to ride Lady Trix, " anyhow, any shape," and to that sensitive animal's perfect satisfaction, which, in such a case, was far more important than the satisfaction of her master.

" But, my little girl, what shall we say to the people at home ? What will they think of me as a guardian for their jealously-loved child ?"

Steenie sat thoughtful for a moment; then her face cleared. " They 'll say I ought to do it if I can, — that is, if he was here to know 'bout it my father would say so. He tells me all the time to show my 'preciation of your kindness; an' how am I going to if you don't let me have any chance ? The only one way I can do things for you is through your horses, 'cause I know 'bout 'em. Is n't it ? I 'm puffectly sure my father would say yes."

The Judge was reasonably certain of that also; but he was not so positive concerning Madam's opinion. However, his inclination urged him so strongly that he at last replied : " Then, my brave, helpful little girl, hear me. If I let you ride you

must take the thousand dollars I offered. Wait —
listen — understand.   It is the want of just that
paltry sum which necessitates your grandmother's
leaving her old home ; she was ' short ' just that
amount in her indebtedness, or 'liability,' after
the farm was sold.   To raise this money she is
to sell her home.   She would not accept the loan
of it, because she saw no way of ever repaying
it ; and if your dear father's writing ever comes
to anything, it will be in the future, — some
distance.

" If you ride and win the race you must consider that you earn the money fairly; and must
take it.   Else — no — decidedly — to the whole
proposition."

Again Steenie considered seriously.   Her hesitation was not for herself, of course, but for that
proud old lady whom she so loved and, also,
feared.   " If I earned it that way it could n't be
wrong, could it ?   To keep a dear grandmother
in ' the home of her youth.'   My father says
what we do things for, makes the things hono'ble,
or dishono'ble.   That was 'bout the riding-school.
He would have let me, only he did n't like —
You know. 'Count o' Grandmother.   This won't
be wrong, will it ? "

" From my point of view it seems very right,

in every way ; unless you are afraid of the horse,
or the publicity."

" What 's that ? "

" The people, — the being stared at. Will it
make any difference with your nerves ? "

" No ! Oh, no ! Grandmother says I have n't
any nerves, she guesses. And I 'm not afraid of
folks — no more than horses. Why should I be?
They 're awful nice to me. Everybody is."

" How can they help being ? Is it a compact,
then ? "

" Yes, yes, yes ! Oh, what fun ! It makes
me think of San' Felis' an' my dear ' boys,' an'
most of all of darling Bob. He 'd be proud of
the Little Un, would n't he ? Oh, if he only
knew ! " She turned from Trixie's stall toward
the stable-door, and looked up at somebody
who stood there, the attendant groom, she had
supposed.

" He does, Little Un ! Here he is ! All the
way from Californy to see you win ! "

" Bob ! My Bob ! "

CHAPTER XVI.

WHAT? What is this?" Judge Courtenay looked incredulously around; and there was Steenie clasping her arms about the neck of a tall stranger who had knelt upon the stable floor, the better to receive her caress,

STEENIE AND LADY TRIX.

and whose brown, honest face shone with a delight which matched her own. "Bob, is it? Why, sir, I know all about you! And right glad I am to see you."

"The same, sir. Judge Courtenay, I presume. Just got in from the West. Hunted up the 'boss' first, and he shipped me on here. Knew it would n't do to keep my eyes from the sight of this here young lady, not no longer 'n necessary, no."

"Oh, Bob, why did n't you send me word so that I could have been 'xpecting you? I'm so glad — glad — glad!"

"Glad I did n't, hey? But you've growed! You've growed a power sence I lifted you aboard cars at San' Felis' station. How's ever'thing?"

"Everything? Well. No — I don't know. Did Sutro Vives get safely back home?"

"Yes; Sutry's all right," answered the Kentuckian, quietly, and fixing a significant glance upon Judge Courtenay's face. "But let me in on this racket. What is it? A horse-race, eh?"

"Yes; and I'm to drive and ride this beauty. I must win, Bob! I must. But now I know I shall — with you on hand to 'courage me. Oh, I'm so glad, so glad!"

"Give me the hull business. What's about this thousand dollars?"

"Down here, — sit right down here, an' wait till I tell you." Down sat the ranchman, obediently, and Steenie close beside him, while she poured into his ears a rapid history of what had befallen her since her departure from her childhood's home.

Much of this he had already learned from her letters; much more Sutro had told him; but this last threatened calamity — the family moving on

the morrow from the old house in High Street to
the tiny cottage in the suburbs — and the priva-
tions which menaced this child so dear to him,
was news and sad news. Still, he had come East
to put his own powerful shoulder to the burden
his beloved Little Un was so bravely trying to
lift with her own childish strength, and there
"was no such word as fail" in Kentucky Bob's
vocabulary.

"Well! Where's yer rig-out? Ain't a goin'
to 'pear afore the assembled multitudes in just
that flimsy frock, are you, — or is it a new
style?"

"No! Course not. Did I ever? But I've
the cutest little habit 'at ever was! Grandmother had it made for me; 'cause Mary Jane
said, 'If I was bound ter break my neck, I'd
better break it lookin' 'spectable.' Oh, that
Mary Jane! She's the dearest, best, funniest
little old body; moves all of a jerk, an' so quick
she makes Mr. Resolved dizzy to watch her, — so
he says. He's way down, down at the bottom
of everything, all the whole time; but he has
the lumbago, an' it's that I s'pose. Though
she's his sister an' she does n't get hypoey, never.
An' — oh, my habit? Why, you see, dear Bob,
when we had to sell Tito — "

"Wh-at? Say that again. 'Pears like I don't understand very sharp."

"Did n't I tell you 'bout that? But it was so. We could n't 'ford to keep him, my grandmother says; an' Judge Courtenay bought him; an' Papa put the money in the savings bank toward my education, 'cause he said it was a'most like takin' money for folks, an' it should n't be used 'cept for the best purpose. And dear Mrs. Courtenay made me bring my habit an' keep it here; so 's when I 've done my lessons extra well I can have a ride on Tito for a 'reward.' Anyhow, I see him every day; an' I 've 'xplained it to him best I could; but he does n't understand it very well, I think. Any way he does n't behave real nice. When I go away he whinnies an' cries an' acts — he acts quite naughty, sometimes. But he ought n't; for everybody is as good as good to him. Come and see him this minute."

Away went the reunited friends, and Tito's intelligent eyes lighted with almost human joy when his kind old instructor laid a caressing hand upon his head, and cried out gayly: "Howdy, old boy! Shake, my hearty, shake!"

Up went Tito's graceful fore-leg, and "shake" it was, literally and emphatically. When this ceremony was over and the magnificent stables

of Rookwood had been duly examined and ad-
mired, Steenie was commissioned to bring her
friend into dinner, which was early that day on
account of the afternoon's arrangements. During
its progress, Bob managed to give considerable
information concerning Santa Felisa happenings,
as well as dispose of a hearty meal. He had
" begged off " from going to table with " these
high-toned Easteners; 'cause you know, Little Un,
't I never et to no comp'ny table nowheres, — not
even to your 'n an' your pa's. I 'm a free-born
American, an' all that rubbish — but I know
what 's what : the more for that reason. In —
my place I 'm as good as the next feller an'-a-
little-better-too-sir; but outen it — I 'm outen it.
Them 'at rides the plains an' looks arter stawk,
as I 've done the last hunderd years, more or
less, hain't learned to dip their fingers into no
fingerbowls nor wipe their mustache on no fringed
napkins."

But Judge Courtenay overruled the stranger's
objections, and once having accepted the situation, Bob made the best of it. He was awkward,
of course, and ignorant concerning table etiquette;
but he let his awkwardness apologize for itself by
his simple good nature in the matter; and if his
talk was not polished, it was full of wit, origi-

nality, and a verve that carried his listeners captive.

"Well!" said Mrs. Courtenay, when at last they could no longer delay their rising from the board, "I do not know when I have enjoyed anything so much as your descriptions of ranch-life. It is almost as good as seeing it for myself; and it gives me a real longing for its breeziness and freedom from social cares and restrictions."

"It 's the only life worth livin', ma'am, in my opinion. Which same I don't go for to set up ag'in that of any other man or woman, only for myself. I — I could n't exist anywheres elst, for any great length o' time. I don't want nothin' less 'an a ten-mile field to swing my long arms round in. There ain't — But, what 's the use? If I talked all day I could n't tell nobody what them big open spaces o' airth an' sky is to me; an' if they 's a good Lord anywheres about, He 's out there in them blossomin' plains an' snow-capped mountains an' etarnal sunshine.

"My old Marm uset ter sing 'bout the ' Beautiful Heaven above,' an' 'pear to enjoy thinkin' on 't; an' once I ast her what she 'lowed it was like. She said if 't was like anything she knowed, she 'd ruther it 'd be like Salem village, — out hum in the State o' Massachusetts, — an' ary other place she 'd ever seen. But I don't want no villages in mine; an' if ever I git thar I don't ask no purtier place 'an Californy to go ridin' round in, forever an' ever. Amen."

"Ah! Well, to most of us, probably, Heaven is typical of what we like best," said the Judge, gravely, and led the way library-ward. Where, for a while, he held a most absorbing conversation with this stranger from the West; and when it was ended his genial countenance was even more serious than before.

Then came the shouts of the children, eager to be off to the "course;" and thither, presently, everybody repaired.

"Well, Little Un, you look prime! Bless my eyes! 'Pears ye 've growed more 'n five months' wuth, in these five months o' time, long as they has be'n to old Bob, without ye. An', huckleberries! They is quite a crowd around, ain't they! Well, you don't mind that none, do ye?"

"Why, of course not; an', Bob, let me tell you, you stand in some certain place, — you pick out where, — an' every time I go round I 'll look at you, see? Then you can make all the old signs you used to make, an' it 'll be a'most as good as Santa Felisa. But, think of it! A

thousand dollars! I want to win just as much.
I truly do. Don't I? If only for Judge Courtenay's sake, 'cause he's so dear an' kind, an' he's
Beatrice's papa, — an' I love her so very, very
much. But most of all, now — an' it grows
more an' more so — I wish to get that money so
my darling old grandmother won't have to leave
her own home an' her pretty library, nor anything. Oh, do you think I'll do it?"

"Sartain. Sartain as I live. But you an'
I've got a job to tackle arterwards. Look at
these horses round here! Did ye ever see sech
a lot o' poor, tortured, mis'able critters? Look
at that check-strap yonder! The man 'at owns
the poor thing 'pears quite peart an' quality-like,
but he's a fool all the same. Wish I could hitch
a string to his front lock o' hair an' yank his
idiotic old head over back'ards, same way! Bet
he wouldn't go trot, trot, round that peaceable.
No, siree, he'd yell like a painter, an' smash
things if he couldn't get loose. An' that other
nincompoop further down that way, see that
breechin' he's put on his horse? He'd oughter
be shot, 'cause big's the world is thar ain't room
enough in it for sech idiots as him! If I was
that horse I'd set right down on that strap an'
go to sleep, I would."

" Oh, you dear old scolder!   You'll see lots o'
cruelty to horses here in Old Knollsboro; but
the folks don't understand 'em as well as you an'
I do.   That's the reason.   My father says it
is n't 'tentional unkindness, it's only ignorance.
Ah!   There they are calling me.   Come!"

The news had spread that Judge Courtenay
had found a jockey to ride his Trix, and one who
was to drive her in the trainer's place; so the
spirit of his wealthy opponent sank a little.
However, an untried, unpractised assistant, as
this new hand must be, was quite as liable to
lose as win the contest for his employer, even
though the animal he rode was unequalled for
speed. ₁ This second thought sent a thrill of satisfaction to the heart of Doctor Gerould, the master of Rookwood's rival, and he now felt confident
of his own success.   Like his friend, the Judge,
he was warmly enthusiastic over his "hobby,"
and would, in the height of his excitement, have
gone to any honest length to carry off that day's
laurels.

But when, after some preliminary contests
between inferior beasts, the real one began, and
the four thoroughbreds who were to compete for
the famous "Rookwood cup" were drawn into
line at the starting place, he saw the girlish little

17

figure which was lifted into the sulky behind Trixie, his courage ebbed again.

"That child! Why how in the world did he obtain her family's consent!'" exclaimed a neighbor.

"No matter how; there she is."

"But, have confidence, sir. She's only a girl. She cannot have the wisdom and skill —"

"Cannot she? Maybe you have n't heard about her; though, was n't it yourself expatiating upon her wonderful riding over our country-roads on her piebald mount? Why, man alive, the child 's a witch! So they claim; and — Jupiter! If they have n't imported a regular 'Wild Westerner' besides! Well, I might as well give it up. Mordaunt 's beaten."

Kentucky Bob was moving about Trixie as she stood waiting, examining every strap and buckle of the light harness she wore, testing its strength and that of the skeleton-like vehicle in which he had placed his beloved "Little Lady of the Horse." His gaunt face was grave and anxious. He did not like this experimenting with untried animals, and at such a stake. Still, he knew the mettle of the driver if not the steed, and his superstitious faith in Steenie's ability to succeed everywhere and in everything made his words cheerful, if not his heart wholly so.

"I come jest in time, did n't I, Little Un? An' don't you get excited an' ferget. You take the outside. Thar ain't no legs in this show 'cept Trixie's an' that Mordaunt's thar. Them two other critters 'll drop out in no time; then you jest keep a steady head — an' hand — *an' the outside!* Don't you ferget it. I ain't a goin' to have ye crowded up ag'in no railin' an' so caught an' beat — mebbe hurt. Keep to the outside, though they be so p'lite as ter offer ye the inside show. Steady, is the word. Go it slow — warm her up — put on steam — get in ahead. Thar ye go! Californy to win!"

But not so easily. It was a contest hardly, barely won. Yet it was won — and honestly; and, the driving over, Steenie was swung to the ground once more by her attentive Bob, who was far more pleased and proud than she.

"Ye did it, Little Un! Ye did it! Though, o' course, I did n't expect nothin' else o' my 'Mascot'!"

But the child's face was downcast. The cheers and plaudits which followed her as she went into the waiting-room were almost unheard and quite unnoticed, and she bounded toward Judge Cour-

tenay with actual tears of vexation in her blue
eyes. " Oh, I 'm so sorry ! You 'll never have
any faith in me again, will you ? "

" Why, my dear little girl ! You 've won !
Did n't you know that you had won ? " cried
the master of Rookwood, in high delight.

" Call it ' won,' sir ? That little bit o' ways ?
Trixie should have been in a dozen lengths ahead,
'stead of just a teeny, tiny bit ! I 'm so sorry,
so sorry ! "

That was the only way in which she could be
induced to regard her victory ; but when, later
on, the riding was announced, her vivacity and
hopefulness returned. " Now — I 'm all right !
I can ride — anything ! Same 's I can breathe,
just as easy. An' see here, my Lady Trix, you
have got to 'xert yourself this time, you dear,
beautiful, lazy thing ! You hear ? If you don't
I 'll never speak to you again as long as I live !
So there, my dainty one ! "

Whether Trixie understood, who can tell ?
Certainly the dire calamity her small friend
threatened was not destined to befall the proud
queen of Judge Courtenay's stables. Maybe
because riding was, as Steenie said, more natural
to her than driving, it was evident from the word
" Go ! " that she was the winner by long odds.

She kissed her hand to Beatrice. — PAGE 261.

Almost it seemed, toward the last, that there was practically no contest at all ; but the truth was that such wonderful equestrianship as Steenie Calthorp accomplished that day had never been seen on that or any other course thereabouts.

"I'm bound to beat! — and beat so far that I'll feel all nice and clean about it in my heart, too!" she declared at starting; then she kissed her hand to Beatrice, watching wide-eyed from a seat of honor, and rode gayly away to victory. With her little face smiling and rosy, yet tremendously in earnest, the far-away look in the bonny eyes, the aureole of sun-kissed ringlets streaming on the air, she seemed to communicate to her mount her very thoughts and feelings, — "For Grandmother and Home!"

It was love, then, that won! — love and unselfishness, which even in the person of a little child were irresistible, as they are always irresistible. And so well she did her part, so noble was her aim, that, now he had learned it, even Doctor Gerould lost every opposing wish.

"Well! well! If that's the case, I'd rather she'd beat than not — of course! — even if it damages Mordaunt's record. And I'll double the price if they'll let me."

"But, of course, also, that can't be, my friend,"
explained the Judge. "It's just as probable as
not that the Calthorp pride will up and make a
rumpus about the whole matter, even now. I
shall feel more comfortable after I know how
the check is received. But if anything was
ever honestly earned that was! — and never
did I draw one so willingly. There they go!
Good luck go with them!"

There they went, indeed! Riding in state
through the streets of Old Knollsboro, in the
Courtenay carriage, with the Courtenay livery.
on the box, and crowds of admiring people, returning village-ward, watching their progress.
Straight from love's triumph to the square white
house in High Street, and to the brilliant smile
of the polished old "lion" on its door, a smile
of welcome Steenie had long since learned to
regard it.

Grandmother Calthorp, sitting sadly at the
window of her beloved and now denuded library,
saw this royal approach, and wondered. Then
her heart chilled with fear lest harm had befallen the child who had grown into its very
depths, and had now become the centre of life to
it, dearer than any other living creature, dearer
even than the precious packed-away books which

had for so long outranked humanity in the Madam's estimation.

But Steenie was not hurt! A second glance showed that; for through the hastily-donned eye-glasses the waiting woman saw that the child had risen in her place, and stood waving joyously above her head a tiny strip of paper, while the sparkling little face proclaimed in advance: "Good news!"

Then the carriage stopped; and, although the bearer of the paper longed to jump out, she restrained herself till the footman had opened the cumbrous door which stayed her impatient feet. Then, out upon the ground and up the path she sped, scarcely touching the ground in her eagerness.

A noisy entrance, truly, but who could help that, or who reprove?

"Grandmother! See here! See here! You need n't move! Never — never — never! A thousand dollars! A whole one thousand splendid dollars! I earned it! I won the race! For you — for you!"

Then the white paper fluttered into the trembling old hands; and Steenie's dancing feet bore her swiftly from the room to find and share with the proud father her happy news.

CHAPTER XVII.

CONCLUSION.

RESOLVED AND MARY JANE.

*L*AND o' Goshen! Madam 's a cryin'!" Mary Jane had rubbed her eyes repeatedly, believing they deceived her; but she was now forced to admit the truth of their report.

" 'T ain't no sech a thing!" retorted Resolved, testily. Yet he advanced to peep over his sister's shoulder at this startling phenomenon; then he pushed his spectacles up out of place, the better to "see with his own eyes" this unprecedented proceeding, and ejaculated : " My-soul-I-declare!"

This was what he beheld.

Daniel Calthorp sitting near the window, leaning his brow upon his hand, not indeed to veil his sightless eyes from any untoward spectacle, but to hide the workings of his own face.

Kentucky Bob standing in the doorway, uneasily shifting his great length from foot to foot, and ready for flight the instant things became "a trifle too tropercal fer a Westerner."

While Steenie was kneeling before the Madam's chair, her warm little hands resting upon the worn white hands in the lady's lap, and her eager, loving glances trying to interpret the conflicting emotions which pictured themselves upon the noble face above her.

The worst sign of all, in Mary Jane's opinion, was that her proud mistress evidently did n't even care how many witnessed this unusual display of weakness. "She ain't a tryin' ter hide nothin'! Not a tear! Poor soul, poor soul! She's a down deep in the waters o' triberlation when she lets go o' her hefty sperrit, an' don't mind us a seein' what we do now. That ever I should a lived ter look at Madam Calthorp a weepin' tears! Oh, my soul, oh! I did think 'at we'd manage ter go out the old house, as Steenie says, 'colors flyin'' an' hearts braced up, even if bust. But when she — *she* — gins out, let us *all* gin out. Oh, me — me!"

"Shat up carn't ye? Hark! What 's the youngun a sayin' ? "

Curiosity comforted the faithful old serving-woman's immediate grief; she paused in the very middle of a sigh to listen.

"Don't look so, dear grandmother, darling grandmother! Did I do so very, very wrong? Do b'lieve me, I did n't mean to. An' — my! Wait, Grandmother! If you don't want it, please don't cry on poor Judge Courtenay's check, 'cause Papa says — Oh, Grandmother! Will you? Will you ? "

The pantomime was more intelligible than the words. For the first time the stately head was bent slightly, — even under the relaxation of these unprecedented circumstances it had been held upright, — and a sudden smile broke over the tear-wet face, making it beautiful as proud.

Proud it had always been, but not as now, proud with an unutterable tenderness, proud — even that paradox — in a new, sweet, and reverent humility, as the thin hands gently dropped upon the child's curly head, and the tremulous lips found voice: "Steenie, Steenie! My brave, precious one! Hush! There is no reproach for you; there is nothing but love and obligation. You have humbled me as I have never been humbled in my life; and you have made me proud as I have never been proud. You have conquered your grandmother, now come to her."

Steenie leaped, joyfully, into the arms opened to receive her, but the words which had fallen from the Madam's lips mystified her, and she was still clinging about the speaker's shoulders, looking doubtfully upon the narrow white check, which had fallen to the carpetless floor, when Bob's resonant voice cut into a scene which was becoming " too all-fired watery round the eyes for him," and cleared the mystery.

" Which means, my Little Un, begging your pardon, Ma'am, an' everybody's pardon, that our ' Little Lady of the Horse ' hain't won her ticket for nothin'. Which bein' the case — I say, old feller? You Unresolved old Puritan, you, I think I know a cure for your lumbago. Want to hear it ?"

" Yes, yes," answered Mr. Tubbs, eagerly.

" Here 't is. Price nothin'. Turn to an' fetch a hammer an' nails, an' unroll that strip o' carpet thar. I don't relish the sound o' my own boots on hard oak floors like this un, an' the sooner we get the carpet back into place, the sooner I shall feel to hum. Lively, now. We 'll get it down afore pitch-dark, even in this region o' short days."

To picture Mr. Tubbs's disgust is impossible. Then, even to his selfish heart, crept a warm, tender, human feeling, and he cast a sidelong glance at the mistress he had served so long, if not so well.

Observing which, Bob, that clear-sighted translator of people's emotions, gave friendly encouragement. "That's the fust step. Second — look! See here? Look at this vial? Know what it is? Ever see anything so fine?"

"Eh? No. What is it?" demanded Resolved, who had a keen eye and ear for anything in the shape of "medicine."

"Rattlesnake ile, — that's what she is. Double distilled, an' forty-thousandth purity. Volatile as gas. Can't fix it in no ordinary bottles, with no ordinary stoppers. Worth its weight in gold; worth more if it could n't be replaced. Sample I brought from my Little Un's property, — from the rancho er the mountain o' Santa Trinidad. Hm! Did n't mean to say that — yet. But no matter. Step lively now. An' if ye do, I 'll rub some o' this precious stuff on your worthless old back, an' if I don't bounce the lumbago, my name ain't Bob, an' I hain't never rid on no Santa Felisa round-up."

There was tonic, elixir, in the very tone; not

only for the stiff-jointed Mr. Tubbs, but for every individual there present.

Mary Jane, proper Baptist that she was, almost executed a fancy dance; but recollecting herself in time, went hurrying away to her kitchen, her cracked, quavering, but joyful voice proclaiming in song, —

> " I 've reached a land of corn and wine,
> And all its riches freely mine.
> Here shines undimmed one blissful day,
> For all my night has passed away."

Mr. Calthorp crossed over and gave his mother a grateful kiss, then walked out whistling.

Steenie slipped down and watched her grandmother fold the beneficent scrap of white paper safely away in her pocket-book, then danced a *pas-de-seul* without any of Mary Jane's scruples of conscience.

And even Madam Calthorp began humming softly some melody of her youth, and moved the chairs out of the room, to further the cheerful labor of Kentucky Bob, who had the carpet unrolled and into place, " in the jerk of a lamb's tail," and who whistled gayly, till he remembered that he was the guest of a high-bred lady, when he restrained himself, and worked away all the faster, maybe.

"My, is n't it just too delightful to be happy!" cried small Steenie, in the fulness of her rapture; and the instant laugh which greeted her quaint exclamation was answer sufficient.

"It 's taken ferever ter git these things tore up an' out o' place; but I guess they 'll 'bout fly back inter it ag'in, o' their own accord," said Mary Jane, unwrapping the parlor "table-spread" and recklessly throwing away the string. While Resolved puffed and stretched at that carpet, determined to keep ahead of Bob's resolute, speedy "tack," "tack," without one grunt or groan.

Was n't it fun to put that old house "to rights" once more? Was n't it? Such fun that, as Mary Jane prophesied, the furniture almost seemed to march itself back into position; while Steenie was allowed, not only to handle, but to unpack and restore to their own shelves the precious books which seemed "folks a'most" to their loving owner.

But to all sunshine there is shadow. To the brightest day succeeds a twilight; and a spiritual twilight fell upon these happy people, when, after all was done that could be done, they gathered about the blazing fire on the great hearth-stone in the dining-room, and heard the story which Kentucky Bob had come so far to tell.

" 'Pears as if I did n't know how to begin it. But I must; though I ain't no oraytor, I ain't. Come a here, Little Un. The 'boss' won't mind a sparin' of ye to me I 'low, an' mebbe I kin talk straighter a feelin' yer little hand in mine. Good little hand, strong little hand, lovin' little hand, that takes right a holt o' everybody's heart an' pulls it out o' wickedness an' inter the straight. Pulled old Sutry Vives out o' malice an' murder, ter live a Christian an' die a martyr."

"What? *What?*" cried Steenie, aghast.

"Hush, Little Un, don't! It's 'bout all old Bob kin do, anyhow — an' — Don't make a break in the perceedin's ag'in, if ye kin help it, don't! 'Cause I ain't much uset ter preachin', an' this here — is *'bout* a — *funeral sermon!*"

He needed not to hush any one again, not even when the " sermon " was ended.

"Sutry, he come hum. When he come I happened ter meet him, an' when he stepped out o' the car at San' Felis' I did n't scurcely know him. Some o' his folks lived above a hunderd; but could n't none on 'em ever looked so old as Sutry did that day. An' when I spoke to him an' told him ' Howdy!' he jest stared up inter my face — No matter ! He's square ; squarest man I ever knowed.

"He told me 't he 'd made his will. He 'd gin
ever'thing he got ter the Little Un. 'Everything you 've got?' says I, laughin', harsh like.

"'Yes, La Trinidad.'

"Then I laughed more, but — not long. That
night he ast me ter take a couple o' the boys, an'
go up inter that snake-infested peak with him.
We did n't wanter. Snakes had n't be'n troublesome none, 'long back; but, somehow, thar
warn't no refusin', he looked that queer an'
un-Sutry like. So next mornin' we went; an'
goin' up he told me all the bad news 'bout you
all, an' his way o' changin' it inter good. He 'd
foond out, he thought, 'at Steenie here could n't
'herit till he was dead. He could gin her anything he 'd a mind to; but he knowed nobody
would n't b'lieve none o' his big talk, long as he
lived. But if it was her 'n, out an' out, they 'd
have ter try an' see what this 'heritance was.
He kinder impressed me even then; an' we went
on quite chipper. Killed a few rattlers by the
way, an' went spang up an' up, an' then down
ag'in, inter the very heart o' the mountain.
Then I seed thar 'd be'n some prospectin' done
thar sometime. We found a trail an' we fol-
lered it.

"An' I ain't never laughed at Sutry Vives, ner

La Trinidad property — sence.   What he showed us was enough ter sober a drunken man arter a big spree.

"Then we started hum ag'in ; but, half-way down, Sutry called us ter stop.

"'Boys,' says he, 'ye 've seen what I showed ye.   I picked you three out, 'cause you love the Little Un, an' I kin trest ye.   Sw'ar 'at you 'll be true ter yer trest ; sw'ar ter do the plumb square by the little Seenoreety.'

"You bet we swore ! — all an' more 'n he ast us.   Then we went on ag'in, but Sutry did ʌ t foller.

"'I feel like I 'd like ter stay here a little while alone,' says he ; 'an' if I don't come down in fair season, you kin come an' hunt me up.'

"'Better not,' says I.   But he would ; an' we, each on us, had our dooty ter do, an' so we left him."

There was a long silence, broken, at last, by Steenie, asking softly : "Well ?"

"Well, when I rec'lect that night — I — Huckleberries!   Carn't ye guess it ?   Think o' the squarest thing a feller could do, an' then know he done it, — that poor, laughed-at, despised, weak-witted old Don Sutry !"

"Oh, tell me, Bob, please! My heart's all suffocky, an' I can't breathe!"

"You 'low I could n't rest. I kep' a thinkin' o' that old vener'ble up thar, a takin' his last look at a property 'at had be'n his 'n, er his folks, sence way back — an' the lonesomeness an' all — an' I could n't stan' it. So I started just arter moon-rise, an' clumb up ag'in, callin' myself names all the time fer a fool. An' when I got to the very heart o' the place — thar he lay, sleepin' quiet an' a'most a smilin', — right thar in that den!"

"But you waked him up, Bob? Quick — did n't you?"

"Yes, I did. Perhaps I had a job, though! 'T was a close call fer the old caballero. An' when I 'd rousted him a little, ye should a heered him pitch inter me! 'Cause I would n't let him lay still thar an' die o' rattlesnake bite!"

"Why, Bob? Why should he wish to die?"

"Fer your sake, Little Un; to make you rich an' happy an' ever'thing. An' I 'low the notion was jest as noble as if he 'd be'n let-ter finish it up as he meant."

"Well? The result?" asked Mr. Calthorp, impatiently.

"Well, he 'll live, I reckin; but his old age

won't be not very flourishin' ner green-bay-tree
like. 'T was an even chance, 'bout. I carried
him down on my back, an' thar happened ter be
an old Indian on hand 'at done his level best;
an' he 'll live. So they think.

" But we had a tussle with him, fust. An' not
till Lord Plunkett himself, who had come round
that way ag'in, was lugged inter the room ter
hear the hull story, an' ter promise ever'thing
should be done same as if he died, would
Sutry consent ter take the stuff old Pueblo
forced down his throat. But, to all intents
an' purposes, he was a martyr, Sutry Vives
was."

The graphic story cast over them all an awed
and solemn feeling which made speech seem
impossible. Till, after awhile, a half-charred
stick fell into the coals, and Mary Jane looked
up through her tears. "Greater love hath no
man than this," said she, softly; and even
Resolved failed to sniff.

Finally Madam Calthorp asked: "What was
in the mountain that made it so valuable in the
old Spaniard's eyes?"

"Sunthin', 'at when it's developed — as Lord
Plunkett an' Jedge Courtenay has offered ter
advance the funds fer — 'ill make the Little

Un rich enough ter kindle fires with jest sech checks as she fetched home ter-day."

"But I do not understand."

"Silver, ma'am, silver.   Quality, A   one. Quantity, unlimited.   That's all it was."

THE END.